LAUREL RESCUES THE PIXIES
by Cassie Kendall

Too noisy, too untidy, too clumsy. Laurel is sure that's how the other woodfairies think of her. She simply doesn't belong in the Dappled Woods. So she announces that she's heading off to the pixie village where her friend Foxglove lives. And she just might stay there forever.

But soon after Laurel arrives at the village, disaster strikes. The pixies spot a forest fire heading right for them!

The pixies are ready to pack up their belongings and leave. But Laurel convinces them to stay and fight the fire.

As the flames draw closer, Laurel wonders if she's making a terrible mistake. Will the pixies be able to save the village? Or will they lose their homes—and perhaps even their lives?

STARDUST CLASSICS SERIES

LAUREL

Laurel the Woodfairy

Laurel sets off into the gloomy Great Forest to track a new friend—who may have stolen the woodfairies' most precious possession.

Laurel and the Lost Treasure

In the dangerous Deeps, Laurel and her friends join a secretive dwarf in a hunt for treasure.

Laurel Rescues the Pixies

Laurel tries to save her pixie friends from a forest fire that could destroy their entire village.

ALISSA

Alissa, Princess of Arcadia

A strange old wizard helps Alissa solve a mysterious riddle and save her kingdom.

Alissa and the Castle Ghost

The princess hunts a ghost as she tries to right a long-ago injustice.

Alissa and the Dungeons of Grimrock

Alissa must free her wizard friend, Balin, when he's captured by an evil sorcerer.

KAT

Kat the Time Explorer

Stranded in Victorian England, Kat tries to locate the inventor who can restore her time machine and send her home.

Kat and the Emperor's Gift

In the court of Kublai Khan, Kat comes to the aid of a Mongolian princess who's facing a fearful future.

Kat and the Secrets of the Nile

At an archaeological dig in Egypt of 1892, Kat uncovers a plot to steal historical treasures—and blame an innocent man.

Design and Art Direction by Vernon Thornblad

Donation 3/2001

This book may be purchased in bulk at discounted rates for sales promotions, premiums, fundraising, or educational purposes. For more information, write the Special Sales Department at the address below or call 1-888-809-0608.

Just Pretend, Inc.
Attn: Special Sales Department
One Sundial Avenue, Suite 201
Manchester, NH 03103

Visit us online at www.justpretend.com

LAUREL
Rescues the Pixies

by Cassie Kendall

Illustrations by Joel Spector
Cover Art by Patrick Faricy
Spot Illustrations by Deb Hoeffner

Stardust
CLASSICS

Just Pretend, Inc.
Attn: Publishing Division
One Sundial Avenue, Suite 201
Manchester, NH 03103

Stardust Classics is a registered trademark
of Just Pretend, Inc.

First Edition
Printed in Hong Kong
04 03 02 01 00 99   10 9 8 7 6 5 4 3 2

Publisher's Cataloging-in-Publication
(*Provided by Quality Books, Inc.*)

Kendall, Cassie.
    Laurel rescues the pixies / by Cassie Kendall; illustrations by Joel Spector; spot illustrations by Deb Hoeffner. -- 1st ed.
    p. cm. -- (Stardust classics. Laurel; #3)

    SUMMARY: Laurel thinks her fellow woodfairies consider her too clumsy, so she runs away to the pixie village, and later helps her new friends fight a forest fire.

    Preassigned LCCN: 98-65897
    ISBN: 1-889514-17-9 (hardcover)
    ISBN: 1-889514-18-7 (pbk.)

    1. Fairy tales. 2. Forest fires--Juvenile literature. I. Spector, Joel, 1949- II. Hoeffner, Deb. III. Title. IV. Series.

PZ8.K46Lc 1998   [Fic]
                       QBI98-677

Contents

One Mistake Too Many

rush in hand, Laurel stepped back to study her painting. Unfortunately, she'd forgotten that a pot of paint was standing open at her feet. So she sent a puddle of blue paint splashing across the grass.

"Oh no!" she exclaimed.

Laurel's cry startled Chitters, her chipmunk friend. He woke from his sleep and dashed for safety—right to Laurel. The chipmunk's flight took him through the spilled paint. And by the time he'd settled on Laurel's shoulder, he'd left tracks all over her dress.

Primrose took one look and started to laugh. Soon the other young woodfairies couldn't help but join in.

"It's not funny!" exclaimed Laurel. She turned to glare at her friends. "I just can't do anything right!" she added.

The smiles faded when everyone saw how upset Laurel was.

But that didn't stop Primrose. The young fairy added a perfect dab of paint to her perfect painting. Then she eyed Laurel and sniffed. "I'm not sure which is prettier," she murmured.

1

"Your dress or the ground."

That was it! Laurel dropped her paintbrush, spraying paint on her slippers. Hands on her hips and wings quivering, she announced, "I've had it! I'm tired of being laughed at! I'm tired of getting in trouble all the time! Maybe I'll just leave!"

Primrose stared at Laurel, startled. "I didn't mean—" she began.

"I know what you meant," interrupted Laurel. "I'm too careless and thoughtless and restless to be a woodfairy!"

She started packing up her artwork and paint. No one mentioned that she was spreading blue streaks everywhere. Meanwhile, Chitters had scrambled down from Laurel's shoulder. He sat a few feet away, his tail flicking nervously.

Only gentle Ivy dared to say anything. She could usually get her friend to calm down. "It was an accident, Laurel," she said softly. "No one is blaming you."

"Oh, Ivy," Laurel sighed. "It's not just this. Everything I've done lately has been wrong!"

She thought back over the past few days. Even Ivy had been a little angry with her at one point. It had been so hot all week. One afternoon Laurel had gone wading in the pool by her treehouse while Ivy sat nearby. Laurel had slipped and splashed Ivy—as well as Ivy's brand-new journal.

And late last night, Laurel had awakened the other wood-fairies. She hadn't meant to be rude. She simply couldn't sleep and wanted to play her flute by starlight. Mistress Marigold, who hardly ever scolded anyone, had spoken sharply to Laurel about that.

There had been more accidents and mistakes too. Laurel didn't even want to think about everything that had happened lately.

"I don't belong here in the Dappled Woods!" she exclaimed. "I *am* going to leave. I'm going to go and live with the pixies!"

All the fairies gasped—even Primrose. But before anyone else could say a word, a calm voice came from behind them.

"Why would you want to live with the pixies, Laurel?"

Laurel spun around. There stood the Eldest, the oldest and best-loved woodfairy of all.

Laurel almost wished she could take back her words. She bit her lip and hung her head. Then she thought again about everything that had gone wrong. All at once, the words poured out.

"I don't fit in here," she told the elderly fairy. "No matter what I try, it doesn't seem good enough."

The Eldest smiled a little. "Everybody feels that way sometimes, Laurel," she said.

"I feel that way all the time," said Laurel.

"All the time?" repeated the Eldest.

"Every single minute of every single day," replied Laurel. "Well," she said, "almost every minute. Almost every day."

"It's a big decision, Laurel," said the Eldest. "Maybe you should take some time to think about it. Are you sure you really want to go live with the pixies?"

Laurel looked around the clearing, as if searching for someone else to answer the question. But the other fairies merely stared back in shock. Even Ivy didn't know what to say or do. No fairy ever talked of living anywhere other than the peaceful Dappled Woods. In fact, Laurel was the only fairy in memory who'd left even for a short time.

Then Laurel thought about her friend Foxglove—the only pixie she'd actually met. He never laughed at her. Didn't that prove that she'd fit in better with pixies than woodfairies?

She sighed and answered the Eldest. "I've already thought about it. I really want to go."

"I can't imagine the Dappled Woods without you, Laurel," said the Eldest sadly.

"Nobody will miss me," Laurel insisted. She continued, "Foxglove is coming to visit today. I'll tell him I want to go back to the pixie village with him. I'm sure he'll be happy to take me along."

At least Laurel hoped that her pixie friend would feel that way. She wasn't sure, for she'd never been to his village before.

All the young woodfairies held their breath. Even Laurel. She was sure that the Eldest would say no and that would be the end of it.

To everyone's amazement, the Eldest slowly nodded. "Very well," the old fairy said. "If you feel that way, you should go and stay with the pixies."

Eyes wide and heart pounding, Laurel stared at the Eldest.

The other young woodfairies sputtered. "Leave the Dappled Woods!" "Live with the pixies!" "Forever!"

"Do you really mean it?" whispered Laurel.

"Perhaps a change will be good for you, Laurel," said the Eldest. She paused before adding, "Yes, I think a short visit with the pixies might be just what you need. That is, if Foxglove agrees to it."

A short visit! Laurel let out her breath. At least the Eldest didn't think she should stay away forever! Though *I* may decide to do just that, Laurel thought.

She didn't say this out loud, however. She just nodded and said, "I guess I'll go pack."

Laurel hurried off. She didn't want any more questions or

remarks about her plans. She wasn't sure she even wanted to think about them herself.

But Ivy wasn't ready to give up. She came fluttering behind. "Oh, Laurel," she gasped. "You're not really going to leave, are you?"

"Yes, I am," said Laurel. "The Eldest thinks it's a good idea. And so do I."

"Well, I don't," said Ivy. "I'm sure the Eldest would understand if you changed your mind."

Laurel shrugged. Then she stretched her wings and rose off the ground. Like all woodfairies, she couldn't fly very high or very far. But taking to the air always made her feel better about things.

By now she could hear the roar of Thunder Falls. Soon the falls and the pond came into sight. Laurel flitted to a huge oak tree that grew near the waterfall. Her sunlit tree-house was nestled in the branches high above.

Laurel ignored the ladder and flew up to the porch. Ivy followed, still trying to think of a way to get her friend to stay.

Once inside, Laurel gazed around a bit sadly. She couldn't imagine leaving her lovely home forever. Every nook and corner was filled with something she'd found or made. She'd even woven the beautiful spread and canopy of her bed.

Still, she'd made up her mind to go. So that was exactly what she was going to do!

With a sigh, Laurel gathered up her traveling bag and began packing. She threw in some clean dresses and extra pairs of slippers.

There were other things she couldn't leave behind. Her flute, of course. And her journal and pencil. Like all wood-fairies, she recorded each day's events in her journal. Now there will be plenty to write about, she thought.

Laurel looked around at the things on her shelves. Into the bag went a bright feather she'd found in a bluebird's nest. To that she added a white stone, washed smooth by Thunder Falls, and a clay bowl she'd made herself.

"You're certainly packing a lot of things," noted Ivy. She'd been pacing the floor in silence while Laurel got ready.

"I may be gone a long time," replied Laurel. "And I want to take some gifts for Foxglove's family."

"Oh, Laurel," moaned Ivy. "I'm afraid I'll never see you again."

"Don't worry," said Laurel, giving her friend a hug. "I'll be back. Even if I decide to stay with the pixies forever, I'll come to visit you."

"Stay forever?" exclaimed Ivy. "Please, Laurel! Don't even think that way!"

"Well, I might like it better there," said Laurel.

"Remember the old woodfairy saying," warned Ivy. "The shade always looks cooler under the next tree." In a worried voice, she added, "Besides, this is just supposed to be a visit."

"A visit!" echoed a familiar voice. "Why, you must be talking about me."

Laurel and Ivy whirled around. Outside on the porch stood Foxglove, a wide smile on his face.

The pixie smoothed down his shaggy black hair and straightened his fishskin tunic. "Sorry. I didn't mean to listen in like that," he said. "But it's hot out in the forest today. I was in a hurry to get up here where there's a breeze. So I came scrambling up the ladder without even a hello."

Laurel waved him inside. "You're always welcome. You know that."

As Foxglove stepped forward, his bright eyes lit on Laurel's traveling bag. "You're all ready for an adventure," he remarked. "I didn't know we had one planned!"

"I'm going away for a while," said Laurel.

Foxglove studied her face, noting that she seemed more sad than excited. "Going away?" he echoed. He glanced at Ivy, who only shook her head.

The pixie turned back to Laurel. "Would you like some company?" he asked with a smile.

"Well, actually, I'd *be* the company," Laurel said. "I thought I'd come to stay with the pixies for a while. In your village."

Foxglove's smile suddenly disappeared.

Laurel felt her heart sink. Foxglove certainly didn't act happy about taking her home with him. Maybe he didn't want her around either.

Maybe she wasn't welcome anywhere!

CHAPTER TWO

Foxglove's Invitation

f course, if you'd rather I didn't come, I won't," Laurel added quietly. "It's just that I need a change. The Eldest even said that I should go. Besides, Foxglove, I've never seen your home. And..."

Laurel trailed off. She finished in a mumble, "It was only an idea. I can find somewhere else to go."

"Wait a minute, Laurel," said Foxglove. "I was thinking. Of course you're welcome to come home with me. It's..."

"It's what?" Laurel asked.

"Well," said Foxglove slowly, "I'm not sure you'll like the way we pixies live. You know that we aren't as neat and tidy as the woodfairies."

"You don't understand. That's exactly what my problem is," protested Laurel. "*I'm* not neat and tidy enough to be a woodfairy!"

"There's an old pixie saying," Foxglove warned. "The berries always look sweeter on the next bush."

"That's a lot like an old woodfairy saying," Ivy said.

"Maybe the berries on the next bush really *are* sweeter," Laurel argued. "I won't know until I try."

Foxglove scratched his chin thoughtfully. Then he nodded. "You're right. You should try it." He bowed to Laurel. "Will you be my guest at Old Warren?" he asked.

"Oh, Foxglove!" exclaimed Laurel. "Are you sure?"

"The more I think about it, the better the idea sounds," Foxglove replied. "I've told the other pixies all about you. It's time you met them."

"When can we go?" asked Laurel.

Before Foxglove could answer, they were interrupted by a rustle of leaves. The branches nearby shook, and Chitters jumped onto the porch. Close behind him was Mistletoe the mouse, another of Laurel's animal friends.

Mistletoe sat up, her dark eyes shining. "Where are you going, Laurel?" she asked.

Like Laurel, Foxglove understood the animals. In fact, Laurel had taught him their speech. So now he answered for her. "She's coming to the pixie village with me."

"What about us?" Mistletoe asked.

"Yes, you can't forget us," cried Chitters. "Wouldn't do! Absolutely not! Impossible!"

"Don't worry," said the pixie. "You're welcome too. There's another old pixie saying. No matter how small the burrow, there's always room for a guest."

He grinned at Laurel. "As to when we can leave—how soon can you be ready to go?"

"Actually, I'm already packed," said Laurel.

Foxglove laughed. "Then let's get on our way!"

Ivy got up. "I'll miss you, Laurel," she said. She gave her friend a big hug.

"I'll miss you too," whispered Laurel.

After Ivy left, Laurel took one last look around her peaceful home. Then she turned to Foxglove. "I'm ready," she said. She grabbed her bag and glided to the ground, with Foxglove and the animals following her. The four friends headed uphill, past Thunder Falls.

Before long the travelers arrived at the edge of the Dappled Woods. In front of them stretched the Great Forest. Its huge trees leaned so close together that little sunlight reached the ground.

"Come on," said Foxglove. The animals raced along the trail ahead of him.

Laurel followed more slowly. It wasn't fear that held her back—at least not fear of the forest. She'd been on other adventures out here. But she'd never felt quite like this. She was excited, sad, and worried—all at once.

Maybe it was because things were different this time. Before, Laurel always knew she'd go home at the end of the adventure. Now she wasn't so sure.

At that moment, Foxglove turned and gave her a grin. Laurel couldn't help smiling back. Everything will be all right, she decided. I'll like living with the pixies. And they'll like having me around. Even if I do make mistakes once in a while.

Laurel hurried to catch up with her friend. "Foxglove," she said, "tell me more about your village. I want to know everything."

As they traveled, Foxglove talked happily. He explained again how the pixies had made their home in Old Warren. The rabbits had once lived there. When they moved on, the pixies scavenged the warren. They'd dug out the rabbit holes to make underground homes. It had taken a lot of digging, he told Laurel. After all, pixies were much bigger than rabbits!

"I hope you'll like my family's burrow," said Foxglove with a nervous glance at Laurel. "It's a lot different from your treehouse."

"It'll be fine," said Laurel. "Tell me more."

"Every home is full of things we've made from what we scavenge or trade," he told her. "Wait until you see!"

Laurel smiled. She knew that Foxglove took great pride in his scavenging. There was nothing he liked better than finding something interesting or making a good trade.

That thought made Laurel stop in her tracks. "Foxglove! I brought a few gifts for your family. But I didn't bring things I can trade with the other pixies!"

"Oh, don't worry about that," Foxglove assured her. "Everyone will understand."

Laurel refused to listen, however. To fit in with the pixies, she'd be expected to make trades.

So she started searching the forest for items. That meant they moved a lot more slowly.

"Hurry up, Laurel," called Foxglove after a while. "It's hot and I'd like to get home. Besides, it's getting late."

"Coming!" she shouted, stuffing a shiny rock into her bag. Yet minutes later, she was wandering off again.

Foxglove finally gave up trying to rush her. He sat at the side of the trail with Mistletoe and Chitters. By the time Laurel rejoined them, all three were napping.

"I'm ready!" Laurel announced.

Foxglove's eyes opened. He stared at the patch of sky that showed through the thick leaves. Still looking up, he got to his feet.

"That's odd," he said. He pointed to some birds overhead. They were all flying in the same direction.

"I've noticed a lot of birds going that way," commented

12

Laurel. "I wonder where they're all headed?"

"I can't figure it out," said Foxglove. "They don't usually fly in big flocks like that at this time of year."

He shook his head uneasily. "Well, let's go."

Now they moved more quickly through the forest. Even so, it was late afternoon by the time the travelers reached Old Warren.

Laurel stared curiously around the village. At first she saw only a meadow filled with grassy mounds. Then she noticed that a wooden door was set into the side of each mound.

Laurel realized that the doors must lead into the pixie homes. But she didn't see any sign of the villagers themselves. The meadow was quiet and empty.

Suddenly Laurel spotted a pixie. A small girl was sitting at the entrance to one home. Her eyes lit up when she saw the travelers. At once she jumped to her feet and hammered on the door.

"Everybody! Come here!" she shouted. "Foxglove's home! And he's brought company!"

The little pixie jumped aside as the door burst open. Five more pixies darted out. Then other doors popped open. In seconds, dozens of pixies had surrounded Foxglove and his friends.

Laurel found herself bobbing back and forth in a flood of pixies. They were all very loud—and very excited. In fright, Mistletoe and Chitters jumped into Laurel's traveling bag.

As she looked from one pixie to another, Laurel grew a bit dizzy. So many faces. So many voices. So much noise!

What have I gotten myself into? she wondered.

CHAPTER THREE

Pixie Ways

ll right, everybody! Let's settle down!" shouted Foxglove. In a softer voice, he said to Laurel, "They're just excited about having a visitor."

The noise and confusion died down a bit. But a sea of curious faces still circled Laurel. The pixies were all shapes, she noted, from thin to chubby. They were a wide range of ages too. Gray-haired grandparents stood next to younger adults with babes in arms. And there seemed to be dozens of small, active children.

Laurel felt a tug on her wings. She spun around to find a little pixie dancing up and down behind her. It was the same child who'd first noticed Laurel's arrival.

"Oh, it's you," Laurel said. The little pixie giggled and reached up to pull on the fairy's wings again.

"Okay, that's enough, Tansy!" said Foxglove. As he spoke, he bent over and picked up the small pixie. She threw her arms around Foxglove's neck and grinned at him.

"This is my littlest sister," Foxglove said. "She's an awful pest—as you've already found out." However, his dark eyes twinkled as he held Tansy close. It was plain to Laurel that he loved his little sister dearly.

Foxglove turned to the other pixies. "You've probably guessed who this is," he said. "I'd like you to meet my friend Laurel. She's visiting from the Dappled Woods."

Mistletoe and Chitters peeked out from their hiding place. Foxglove introduced them as well.

As the pixies began to call out their hellos, one stepped forward and bowed. "Welcome to Old Warren, Laurel," he said. "And you're welcome too, Chitters and Mistletoe. Foxglove has told us a lot about all of you. We're delighted to have you visit."

"This is my father, Bramble," said Foxglove proudly. Laurel smiled. She'd guessed as much. Bramble looked like an older copy of Foxglove. Same shaggy black hair. Same friendly grin. Same sparkling eyes.

As she greeted Bramble, Foxglove reached into the crowd and pulled forward a sweet-faced pixie woman. She smiled warmly when Foxglove introduced her as his mother, Buttercup.

"Laurel would like to stay with us for a while," Foxglove explained.

"Only if I won't be a bother," Laurel added hastily.

"A bother?" echoed Buttercup. "Don't be silly, child. A guest is never a bother. We have plenty of room for you."

"What about us?" piped a high voice. "Can we meet Laurel and her friends too?"

Laurel glanced down. Three young pixies—as alike as petals on a daisy—stood in front of her. Each had dark eyes and a crop of wild brown curls. They wore long tunics tops and olive green leggings.

Foxglove laughed. With his free hand, he mussed the curls of the three. "These are my other sisters," he announced. "Posy, Plum, and Petunia."

Laurel wasn't sure which sister was which, so she simply nodded at each. Mistletoe and Chitters squeaked hello as well. However, when a small hand reached for his tail, Chitters ducked out of sight again.

Foxglove went on to introduce many more pixies, all of whom crowded near to meet their guests. Names and faces swirled in Laurel's mind. I'll never keep them all straight, she thought. Especially since they don't hold still for long.

At last Laurel seemed to have met everyone. Families began to drift back to their own homes, continuing to wave to the newcomers.

Foxglove's mother took Laurel's arm. "I'm sure you're hungry after your long trip," she said. "Come and have some dinner with us."

Buttercup didn't wait for a reply. Chattering happily, she led the way to the door where Laurel had first seen Tansy. Foxglove followed, talking to his father and carrying Tansy. His other sisters ran in circles around the group.

At the door, Buttercup paused to show Laurel around the outside of the house. Meanwhile, Foxglove put Tansy down. "I'll be right back," he said. "I'm going to show Mistletoe and Chitters a good spot to stay." The two animals crawled out of Laurel's bag and hopped to the ground.

Foxglove's parents gave Laurel a tour of their vegetable patch. Then they moved on to their packed storage shed. Laurel was admiring everything when Foxglove returned.

Buttercup nodded to her son. "If you'll fetch some water, Foxglove, we can finish making dinner for our guest."

"All right," he agreed. "Follow me, Laurel. I'll show you where the spring is."

As his sisters started after him, he held up a hand. "Not this time. Go help Mama and Papa with dinner. You can visit with Laurel later."

The rest of the family disappeared into the burrow. With a smile for his friend, Foxglove said, "I thought you could do with a bit of peace."

"Your family is wonderful!" Laurel exclaimed. "You're lucky to have so many people who love you."

Foxglove eyed her carefully. "You have lots of people who love you too, you know."

Laurel shrugged. "Maybe," she said. "Still, it's not the same as having a family like you do."

They reached a deep, bubbling pool and lowered the bucket into the clear water. As they started back, a question occurred to Laurel. "You were gone a long time with Chitters and Mistletoe. Was something wrong?"

Foxglove shook his head. "No, not really. Chitters was just a little fussy about where he wanted to sleep."

Back at the door of his house, Foxglove grinned. "Are you ready for this?" he asked. "I'm afraid that dinner at my house is a bit noisier than you're used to."

"I'm looking forward to it," Laurel assured him.

Foxglove smiled again and motioned her down the steps. At the bottom of the staircase, Laurel paused. A neat row of slippers and shoes lay there, heels out and toes pointing toward the wall. Obviously the pixies removed their footwear before going inside.

Foxglove leaned over and took off his shoes. "Put yours with the toes pointing out," he said. "That's what visitors do."

Laurel and Foxglove placed their shoes with the others. Then, parting a curtain, they stepped into a large round room. Like the stairwell, it had been hollowed out of the earth. But the pixies had added many special touches. The dirt walls had been smoothed and swirled in interesting patterns. Colorful flat stones were laid close together to form the floor.

In the center of the room was a large table. Low benches sat at the sides and round stools were at both ends.

Laurel smiled when she saw a set of antlers hanging on the wall. Coats, hats, and scarves hung from the tips. Foxglove had once told her that pixies scavenged old antlers to use as coatracks.

Laurel saw other things she'd expected. Several wooden bowls sat on a cupboard near the table. They held kitchen supplies—nuts, dried berries, seeds, and grains. Polished rocks sat on the floor, propping open doors that led out of the large room.

Some things surprised Laurel, however. She'd thought pixie homes would be dark and closed in. Instead, the burrow was filled with light and air. In a stone-lined fireplace, a bright fire crackled merrily. High overhead, fresh breezes and sunshine poured through wooden shutters in the roof. Thick candles sat on every surface, ready to light the room when darkness fell.

"This is it," said Foxglove. He sounded a bit unsure of himself.

Laurel smiled at her friend. "It's lovely," she said.

"Do you really think so?" asked Foxglove. "You don't mind that it's underground?"

"No," said Laurel, realizing that she actually didn't mind. Foxglove's home was different from her airy home high in the trees. Still, it was bright and colorful. I like my treehouse better, she told herself. But that doesn't mean I can't like an underground home too!

Tansy popped into the room and at once ran to Laurel's side. "Come on, Laurel," she urged. "I'll show you where you can sleep." With that, she turned and darted toward one of the smaller doors.

Laurel looked at Foxglove. "I don't have to stay in your house," she said. "You find a place to sleep outside when you visit me."

Bramble overheard. "Nonsense," he declared. "We pixies always have room for a guest."

Buttercup added, "Anyway, we feel like we know you already. Foxglove has certainly talked about you enough. Now let Tansy show you where you can sleep."

So Laurel followed Tansy, with Foxglove and his other sisters right behind.

The room she entered was a bit smaller than the dining area. Thick tree branches, arranged in pairs, stuck out from the dirt walls. Hanging from these branches were four hammocks.

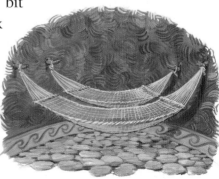

"This is where my sisters and I sleep!" announced Tansy. She opened a huge trunk that sat against one wall. The pixie leaned over, balanced for a moment on the edge, and suddenly slipped inside.

Laurel gasped, but Foxglove laughed. He reached in and pulled Tansy out. The small pixie had another hammock in her hands.

"See? This is for you," Tansy said proudly as Foxglove set her on the floor.

Foxglove took the hammock from his sister and hung it from two empty supports. "There," he said. "You're all set."

"You can leave your stuff here," suggested Posy. At least Laurel thought it was Posy. She really couldn't tell the older sisters apart.

"Thanks," said Laurel, slipping the bag off her shoulder. "But first I have some presents for you."

"Presents?" said four voices as one. As Laurel searched through her bag, the sisters edged closer.

"I brought this for you, Posy," said Laurel as she pulled out the bluebird's feather. "You can use it as a pen."

"Thank you," said Posy. She twirled the bright feather in her fingers, gently stroking the soft tip.

Laurel gave a pretty snail shell to Plum and a stone shaped like a bird to Petunia. Both thanked her.

"What about me? What about me?" begged Tansy.

"Shhh, Tansy! You're being rude," whispered one of her sisters.

Laurel smiled at the littlest pixie. "I know it's hard to wait, Tansy. I feel the same way sometimes." As Laurel reached into the bag, Tansy bounced up and down in excitement.

Laurel pulled out a long rainbow-colored sash. "I made this myself," she said. She tied the sash in a bow around Tansy's waist.

"Oh, thank you!" cried Tansy, throwing her arms around Laurel's neck. Laurel hugged her back. It was a strange feeling, holding someone so small and wiggly. Someone a bit muddy too, she realized.

Bramble appeared at the door. "Time to eat," he called.

"Yes!" cried Tansy. She grabbed the woodfairy by the hand. "Laurel, you can sit by me!"

"Hold on a minute," laughed Laurel. She reached into her bag one more time to find the clay bowl she'd made. Then she let Tansy lead her to the dinner table.

Bramble and Buttercup were delighted when Laurel presented them with the bowl.

"We'll use it at every meal," Buttercup promised. She immediately filled the bowl with berries and set it in the middle of the table.

"Now let's eat," said Bramble. He dipped into a steaming pot that hung over the fire.

"Papa's soup is delicious," Tansy whispered to Laurel.

The little pixie was right. In fact, Laurel had two helpings of Bramble's potato soup. She also ate three slices of the dark bread that Buttercup had baked.

It was more than the food that Laurel enjoyed. She'd never eaten dinner as part of a big family before. Yes, she'd sometimes eaten with Ivy. However, the two of them didn't make much noise—even if Laurel was considered loud for a woodfairy. And the fairies sometimes held great feasts in the Ancient Clearing. But at those meals, they sat quietly and spoke in gentle voices.

Mealtime for the pixies, on the other hand, was filled with noise and laughter. No one seemed to care that crumbs littered the floor and soup dripped on the table.

21

There was lots of teasing—as well as praise. Foxglove's parents thanked each of the girls for something she'd done to help that day. Before long Bramble began to brag about Foxglove and his talent as a scavenger. Buttercup smiled fondly at her son. Even the little girls seemed proud of their older brother.

How nice it must be, Laurel thought. How nice to be part of a family like this.

Dinner was hardly over before Tansy scooted off the bench. She stood behind Laurel, staring at the woodfairy's wings.

"Tansy, leave Laurel's wings alone," warned Foxglove.

"I'm not touching them," said Tansy. She leaned around so she could see Laurel's face. "Do they work?"

"What do you mean?" asked Laurel.

"Can you fly like a butterfly? Like a dragonfly? Like a bird?"

"Not quite that well," Laurel said with a grin. "If you want to come outside, I'll show you what I *can* do."

The whole family slipped on shoes and trooped up the stairs behind Laurel. It was almost dark now, and most of the pixies were in their own homes. Light glowed from open doorways and rooftop windows.

Laurel fluttered her wings. As Foxglove's family stepped back, she rose off the ground and circled the pixies.

The youngsters cheered loudly, and their parents clapped.

"Do it again," Tansy called in an excited voice. "I'll race you!"

Laurel flew a few feet off the ground, with Tansy running along beside her. Laurel went slowly, so the little pixie was able to win the race.

"Again!" cried Tansy.

"No. That's enough for now," said Bramble, scooping up his daughter. "It's bedtime."

In spite of their protests, the four girls were soon snug in their hammock beds.

It had been a tiring and exciting day, so Laurel wasn't far behind them. She swung gently in her strange bed. The only sound to be heard was the soft breathing of sleeping pixies.

Through the open rooftop window, Laurel watched the stars gleam brightly. She thought about Foxglove and how much she enjoyed being with him and his family.

And yet...

The pixie lamps reminded her of woodfairy lights in the Dappled Woods. And Buttercup's sweet voice reminded her of gentle Mistress Marigold.

A strange lump rose in Laurel's throat. Was she homesick? How could that be? She'd come to stay in Old Warren because she didn't fit in with the woodfairies. Here she'd been warmly welcomed by the pixies. They actually seemed to like her just the way she was. Still, Laurel wasn't sure that this was where she belonged.

As she finally drifted off to sleep, a question haunted her. Is there anywhere I can feel at home?

CHAPTER FOUR

Dark Clouds Gather

aurel slowly woke. Eyes still shut, she swung back and forth in her hammock. Things don't seem quite right, she thought. She had a strange feeling that someone was watching her.

Laurel opened her eyes. Tansy's face was just inches from her own.

"Are you going to get out of bed, Laurel?" Tansy asked.

Laurel sat up, yawning as she stretched. "Where is everybody?" she said, taking in the empty hammocks around her.

"We've all been up forever and ever," said Tansy. "I had my breakfast and got dressed and played outside. Then I came in to watch you. But Mama said I shouldn't wake you up. I didn't, did I?"

"No, Tansy," Laurel assured the little pixie. "You didn't wake me. Besides, it's time I was out of bed." She climbed out of the hammock and began searching through her traveling bag.

"What are you looking for?" asked Tansy.

"This," announced Laurel. She pulled out a clean dress and a wreath of flowers. "There," she said after she'd quickly changed. "Now let's go join everyone."

Tansy took Laurel's hand and led her out to the other room. "Mama and Papa fixed your breakfast," she said. "So hurry up and eat."

"Tansy!" said Buttercup. "Leave poor Laurel alone!" She put down a stack of wood next to the fireplace and came over to greet her guest.

"Did you sleep well?" she asked. "Did the girls wake you when they got up? Are you hungry?"

Laurel laughed at all the questions. "I had a wonderful sleep," she said. "No, they didn't wake me. And yes, I'm hungry. But you shouldn't fuss over me. I can take care of myself."

"Nonsense," said Buttercup. "You're a guest. Now please sit down." She motioned toward the table where a bowl of dried fruit and seeds was set out.

Laurel gratefully ate her breakfast. However, when she tried to wash up the dirty dish, Buttercup stepped in. "I'll take care of that," she insisted.

"Can't I help you?" Laurel asked.

"No, dear. Run along with Tansy and have some fun," replied Buttercup.

"Come on, Laurel!" begged Tansy. The little pixie was hopping from one foot to the other—clearly tired of waiting.

Hand in hand, the two hurried up the stairs and outside. Even though the sun was hidden behind dull gray clouds, the air was hot and still.

They found Bramble sitting on a stool, a scavenging bag over one shoulder. Posy, Plum, and Petunia were at his feet, making necklaces from dandelions.

"Have you seen Foxglove?" Laurel asked after saying good morning to everyone.

The pixies pointed to a nearby tree. Foxglove was sitting with his back against the trunk, talking quietly to Mistletoe.

Laurel wandered over to her friends. "Good morning," she said. She looked around for Chitters. When she didn't spot the chipmunk, she asked, "Is Chitters still sleeping?"

Foxglove glanced at Mistletoe. Mistletoe glanced at Foxglove. Finally the pixie said, "No. Chitters is gone. He decided to spend the day exploring the woods."

"He did?" said Laurel. "I'm surprised that he didn't want to stay and visit."

"He'll have time for that when he gets back," said Mistletoe. She gave a sleepy shake of her head and slipped back under a bush.

Laurel frowned, still a bit puzzled. Then she turned to Foxglove. "What are you going to do today?" she asked.

"I'm going scavenging, of course," the pixie replied. "With my mother and father. Today we're taking Posy, Plum, and Petunia along for a lesson. They're just getting started as scavengers."

He headed toward Bramble and the little girls. Laurel tagged along. "What about Tansy?" she asked.

"Oh, she's too little," said Foxglove. "She can show you around Old Warren while we're gone."

"I could come with you," suggested Laurel.

"You're here to visit, not work. Why don't you relax and enjoy yourself?"

It doesn't sound like he wants me to come, thought Laurel. But before she had time to worry about this, Tansy was at her side.

"You're staying here, aren't you, Laurel?" begged the little pixie. "Please?"

Laurel smiled. "I'll stay," she said. "If you promise to show me around."

Then she noticed Tansy's hair. The little pixie had woven dandelions—leaves and all—into her curls.

27

"What's that?" Laurel asked.

"My flower wreath," Tansy declared proudly. "Now I look like you!"

Laurel's smile widened. At home no one understood why Laurel was so different from the other woodfairies. Yet here with the pixies, someone wanted to be just like her.

That thought made it a bit easier to stay behind. As the scavengers disappeared into the forest, Tansy tugged at Laurel's hand. "I want to show you something," she said.

Laurel followed the little pixie back into the house and through another door. This room was long and narrow, with many closets set into the walls. Tansy skipped over to one door and pulled it open.

"This is my very own scavenger's closet," she announced.

Laurel had heard Foxglove talk of his scavenger's closet. It was where he kept all the wonderful things he'd found.

Tansy hadn't really started scavenging yet, so there wasn't much in her closet. However, she was proud of what she did have. Her treasures included a necklace of leaves, a fern fan, and a broken belt buckle.

"This is the best of all," Tansy announced, holding up an empty turtle shell. "A turtle used to live inside this. He moved away, so he didn't need it anymore."

Laurel touched the rough surface of the shell. "It's wonderful."

"I'll trade with you," Tansy offered.

"Trade for what?" Laurel asked curiously.

"Your wings!" said Tansy. "That is, if you don't need them."

"I'm sorry, Tansy. I do need them!" said Laurel, laughing. "Besides, they don't come off. They're as much a part of me as your nose is part of you."

"Oh," said Tansy sadly.

"I've got an idea," added Laurel. "Come with me."

She led Tansy back into the sleeping room. From her traveling bag, she took a needle, thread, and a long silky scarf.

She sent Tansy outside to collect thin branches. These Laurel tied together to make two oval shapes. Then she covered the shapes with pieces cut from her scarf.

"There you are," Laurel said. "A pair of wings of your own. They aren't real, but you can pretend to fly with them."

"They're beautiful!" exclaimed Tansy. She twisted around to see how Laurel had attached the wings to her tunic. Then she cried, "Wait right here!" and ran out of the room.

In moments Tansy was back, carrying her turtle shell. "Here," she said. "It's a trade!"

"Oh, Tansy, you don't need to—"

Laurel cut herself short. She'd been about to refuse. One look at Tansy's worried face changed her mind. Laurel knew she had to treat the offer as a real trade. After all, this is what pixies do, she thought. Their trades were more than just a way to get things they needed. They were also a way of sealing a friendship.

"Thank you," replied Laurel. "It's a good trade."

With that settled, they went outside. Tansy wanted to take Laurel to visit some of the other pixies.

At each home, Laurel placed her shoes with the toes pointing out. So did Tansy, saying, "That's the pixie way, you know."

And at each home, Laurel traded something. One old pixie offered her a small pillow stuffed with dandelion fluff.

30

Laurel presented the pixie with a necklace made of seeds.

Another pixie gave her a sharp stone to use for cutting. In trade, he asked Laurel to play a tune on her flute.

By the end of the day, Laurel's bag was full of things she'd gotten from the pixies. Tansy was delighted at being part of all the trades—and at the chance to show off her wings. She hurried Laurel home to share their news.

They found the whole family there. Soon they all sat down for another loud, happy dinner.

Laurel looked around at the faces of her pixie hosts. Maybe this is where I belong after all, she thought. Maybe I'll stay here forever.

~

Halfway through the next morning, Laurel wasn't so sure. A second night in the hammock had left her a little stiff. She'd felt like a butterfly trapped in a cocoon.

Besides that, there had been no breeze for most of the night. Even with the rooftop windows open, the air had remained hot and stuffy.

And no one seemed to be in a hurry to go outdoors. Tansy flitted about the burrow, pretending to fly. Posy, Plum, and Petunia sang a drawn-out tune, slightly off key. Foxglove and his parents got into a long discussion about their next scavenging trip.

Finally Laurel slipped outside by herself. She took deep breaths of the hot, dry air. Even that felt good after being indoors so long.

A few minutes later, Foxglove climbed up the stairs. His four sisters poured out of the door behind him.

"Well, it's time to be off," announced Foxglove.

"I'll come and help," said Laurel eagerly.

Before Foxglove could answer, Bramble and Buttercup joined them. "We wouldn't hear of it," Bramble said. "In this heat? It won't be fun, I'll tell you. Anyway, you're a guest."

A guest, Laurel thought as she watched them leave. Not a member of the family, of course—just a guest. And one without much to do, she realized. For today it seemed there was no one to visit. All the pixies were busy with their own affairs. Even Tansy had run off to play with her friends. "Not everybody has seen my wings," she'd explained.

Laurel stood at the doorstep, uncertain where to go or what to do. "I guess I'll see what Chitters and Mistletoe are up to," she said to herself. She headed for the bushes at the edge of the village, calling her friends' names.

A small nose poked out from under the branches. "Oh, good morning, Laurel," said Chitters. "Greetings. Good day." His words were lost in a huge yawn.

"Where's Mistletoe?" asked Laurel when the mouse didn't appear.

"Off somewhere. Out and about. Exploring," reported the chipmunk. "She'll be back later." With that, he curled into a ball and fell asleep.

Laurel stood up with a sigh. A strange feeling came over her. I'm lonely, she thought.

She remembered what Mistress Gooseberry, her art teacher, sometimes said. "There's no excuse for feeling sorry for yourself," the crabby woodfairy would scold. "The best cure for being out of sorts is to get busy."

Laurel decided that was good advice. "I'll use this time to write in my journal," she said.

She returned to the burrow to get her traveling bag. She

also scooped up a handful of nuts and berries for her lunch. Once outside, she chose a spot under a huge oak and settled down.

Tapping her pencil against her bottom lip, Laurel thought for a while. Finally she started to write.

> The pixies have been very kind to me. Everyone treats me like an honored guest.

What next? Laurel wondered. She didn't want to put down that she was lonely. Or that she was a bit...well, bored. Not when everyone was being so nice.

As Laurel thought, her eyes traveled from one end of the village to the other. A group of youngsters splashed happily at the edge of the spring-fed pool. A few adults were picking berries. Others were cooking, gardening, or mending bags and clothing. All the while, scavengers came and went along the path into the forest.

Laurel ate her lunch as she watched all the activity. Afterwards she wrote a bit more in her journal. Finally, worn out by the heat, she fell asleep in the soft grass.

It was late afternoon when Laurel woke. She noticed that the sky had grown even grayer. There seemed to be a storm brewing in the west.

As Laurel studied the dark clouds, loud cries caught her attention. Another flock of birds was flying high overhead. This wasn't the first such flock she'd seen today, she realized. Nor was it the first to come from the west. Though the birds were too distant for Laurel to hear clearly, their calls sounded worried.

A happy whistle along the forest path drew Laurel's attention back to earth. It was Foxglove—a full scavenging bag

33

hanging from one shoulder. Mistletoe scampered along at the pixie's feet.

Laurel stuffed her journal and pencil into her bag and rose to greet them. "Hello!" she called. "I didn't know you were together."

"We ran into one another a few minutes ago," explained Foxglove.

"Yes," added Mistletoe. "I've been exploring."

At once the mouse bid Laurel good-bye. She vanished into the bushes to join the still-sleeping Chitters.

Laurel shook her head. "I've hardly seen either one of them since I've been here. They always seem to be napping or off in the forest."

"They're on holiday too," Foxglove reminded her. "Now come on inside and I'll show you what I scavenged today. The rest of the family will be along in a few minutes."

Whistling again, the pixie led the way into his burrow. Laurel sighed and followed.

〜

During dinner that night, Laurel felt tired and upset. I might as well go home, she thought.

True, she hadn't made any mistakes. She hadn't had any accidents. But that was probably because she hadn't *done* anything. While the pixies were wonderful, it was plain that she wasn't needed here.

Later, as Laurel lay awake in her hammock, she came to a decision. Early the next morning, she'd announce that she planned to leave. She wasn't sure that she really wanted to go yet. However, she couldn't spend her life as a guest.

Laurel finally drifted off to sleep. All too soon, she was wakened by a banging overhead.

A voice called through the rooftop window. "Buttercup! Bramble! Get up and come outside! Something strange is going on!"

Groaning sleepily, the whole family tumbled out of their hammocks and hurried up the stairs. Laurel followed right behind. They joined a large crowd of pixies, all staring toward the west. Although it was past midnight, the sky glowed a dirty red.

"How wonderful!" Tansy cried with a clap of her hands. "The sun didn't go down!"

"That isn't the sun," whispered one old pixie in a shocked voice. "That's fire!"

CHAPTER FIVE

Hard Choices

ire?" echoed another voice.

The frightening word raced from pixie to pixie. "How far away is it?" someone asked.

"It's still miles off," answered the old pixie who'd spoken earlier. "But the wind is blowing it right toward Old Warren."

"How soon..." one pixie began. He couldn't finish the question.

"Not long," the old pixie grunted. "I'm afraid the fire will reach us in a day or so."

"That explains why the birds have been flying this way!" Laurel whispered to Foxglove. He nodded, his eyes fixed on the distant glow.

"Surely the stream will stop it?" someone suggested.

The old pixie shook his head. "I doubt it. Not with a fire that big. It could jump right across a narrow section of the stream. Or sparks could float across and set another part of the forest on fire."

With a gloomy sigh, the old pixie turned and walked off to his burrow. Others followed, speaking in worried voices as they trotted off to their homes. Finally only Foxglove and his family were left.

"What are they doing?" asked Laurel. "They can't hide from the fire."

"They're not hiding," explained Foxglove. "They're packing up and getting ready to leave."

"We'd better do the same thing," said Bramble. He picked up Tansy and called to the other girls.

"You're not really going to leave, are you?" protested Laurel.

"We have no choice," Foxglove's father replied. "Even underground, we wouldn't be safe from a fire. And after the fire goes past, Old Warren won't be fit to live in anyway."

"Where will you go?" Laurel asked.

Bramble scratched his ear. "It's hard to say," he answered. "We'll wander around the forest for a while, I suppose."

"Sooner or later, we'll find a new place to live," said Buttercup.

"Will it be as nice as Old Warren?" asked Laurel.

Both Bramble and Buttercup looked around sadly. "No, I don't imagine it will be," said Buttercup in a choked voice. "This is the nicest home we've ever had!"

"Then why should you leave?" argued Laurel. "Why don't you stay here and fight for your homes?"

"Fight? Fight how?" asked Bramble, dumbfounded.

"How can anybody fight a big fire?" added Foxglove.

"The pixies must have done it before," Laurel insisted. "Perhaps some of your oldest people would know."

"I don't think so," said Bramble. "When there's trouble, we generally move on."

An expression of hope flashed across Foxglove's face. "What about the Chronicles, Laurel?" he asked. "Maybe there's something about forest fires in there."

Laurel thought about what Foxglove said. The wood-fairies had always kept a written history of events in the Book

of Chronicles. Each year at a celebration, they would read a small part of that history aloud. Though Laurel had never heard a fire mentioned, there were many pages in the Chronicles. And the woodfairies were an ancient people. Surely they had fought a fire sometime in their long past.

Laurel knew what she must do. "I'm going to go back to the Dappled Woods," she announced. "Foxglove may be right. With the Eldest's help, I'll check our records. Whatever I discover about fighting fires, I'll bring back to you."

Foxglove nodded, though the others looked doubtful. They seemed even more so when Laurel added, "In the meantime, you can gather everyone together."

"I don't understand. What's the good of that?" Bramble asked.

"You should have a meeting," answered Laurel. "To decide what's best to do. That's what woodfairies do when there's a serious problem."

"A meeting?" repeated Buttercup.

Laurel sighed, though she wasn't really surprised. Foxglove had been amazed when he discovered how the woodfairies talked things over as a group. He'd told her that pixie families liked to live near one another. However, every family decided what to do and when to do it. They never made plans as a community.

"There's no way one family can fight a fire alone," Laurel explained. "If you want to stay here, you'll have to work together."

Buttercup and Bramble traded glances. "I want to stay," Buttercup declared.

Bramble nodded. "Me too. Let's give it a try."

A round of cheers went up from their children.

"I'm going to get everyone together right now!" Foxglove announced.

He dashed off and began knocking on doors. At each one he called, "Come out! We need to talk."

In response, pixies again gathered outside their doors. Some were already carrying bags stuffed with belongings. All looked sad and worried.

"What's the yelling about?" grumbled one pixie. "Talk, talk, talk! What's to talk about?"

"Nothing," a second pixie protested. "This is wasting time. My family has to get packed if we want to leave at first light." He started back to his burrow.

"Don't go!" yelled Buttercup.

The pixies froze, then slowly turned to stare at Foxglove's mother. Gentle Buttercup wasn't known for shouting.

Foxglove took his mother's hand and led her to the top of a grassy mound. "Listen to her," he begged. "We might be able to come up with a plan."

There was some muttering from the pixies. Nervous eyes moved toward the glow in the west. Feet shuffled back and forth, and bags were shifted from one shoulder to the other. Still, everyone waited to hear what Buttercup had to say.

"Maybe we do have a choice," began Buttercup softly. Her voice grew louder and stronger. "Maybe it's time to stay and fight. To work together to save our homes."

"If we stay, the fire will destroy us," shot back one pixie.

"Stay? Of course we can't stay," another muttered. "What an idea!"

"It's not right to force us to do this!" came a shout.

Bramble joined Buttercup on the mound. "No one is trying to force you to do anything," he said. "We're just asking you to think things over."

He continued, "Our last village wasn't nearly as nice as this. Who knows what we'll find next? Or how long we'll have to wander the forest before we can settle down again?"

Buttercup reminded the others of how happy they'd been in Old Warren. The pixies listened carefully, yet most looked uncertain.

Laurel realized that the discussion might continue a while. And at this point, she didn't dare wait.

She made her way to Foxglove. "I've got to go," she whispered. "Otherwise, I won't have time to check the Chronicles and get back before the fire reaches the village."

"I don't like the idea of you traveling alone at night," said Foxglove. "I'm coming with you."

"You can't," said Laurel. "You need to stay and help your parents. Try to get the others to think about their choices. Maybe they will choose to fight. If so, ask them to wait until I get back with news about how to do that."

"You shouldn't head off by yourself," Foxglove argued. "Someone should go with you."

"I'll go!" said Mistletoe, popping up from behind a pixie foot.

"Me too!" chimed in Chitters. "Absolutely! Certainly! Without a doubt!"

"You see?" said Laurel to Foxglove with a smile. "I have plenty of help. We'll be back as soon as possible."

"I hope we'll still be here by then," said Foxglove. "I can't promise anything. If everyone else leaves, my family will have to go as well."

"I understand," said Laurel.

She reached down to pick up Mistletoe. With the mouse on her shoulder and Chitters dashing right beside, Laurel fluttered away. Ahead of her was the dark, gloomy forest. Behind her, beyond the pixie village, was the glow of the approaching fire.

CHAPTER SIX

A Dangerous Answer

aurel's eyes gradually grew used to the dark. A full moon offered some light, and the stars added their own faint sparks.

As she hurried down the path, a sudden thought almost brought Laurel to a stop. Until now she hadn't even considered the danger to the woodfairies. What if the fire couldn't be stopped? Would it burn all the way to the Dappled Woods?

She hoped not. And it didn't seem likely. The wind would have to change direction for that to happen.

As Laurel sped on, her eyes darted from side to side. The Great Forest seemed so frightening at night! She'd often taken moonlit walks through the Dappled Woods. There it didn't matter if you couldn't see well. Nothing was dangerous. But here shadowy shapes lined the path and strange noises came from every direction.

What is that rattling in the branches above? she wondered. A bobcat ready to leap? And the rustling in the grass. Is it a snake waiting to strike?

Laurel began to move even faster—sometimes flying, sometimes running. She could tell that Mistletoe and Chitters were nervous too. The mouse clung tightly to her shoulder. Chitters scampered by Laurel's side, quiet for once.

As uneasy as they all were, they didn't speak of their fears.

And as tired as they were, they didn't suggest resting. Each knew what was at stake.

By the time they reached the Dappled Woods, dawn had arrived. A pale light lit the familiar scene, and some of Laurel's nervousness vanished. In its place, a terrible tiredness crept over her. If only she could sleep for a while!

Chitters voiced her thoughts. "Shouldn't you stop for a moment? Rest? Catch your breath?"

Laurel shook her head. "I can't, Chitters. I've got to reach the Eldest. Every minute counts. But you two can—"

"We'll stay with you," Mistletoe interrupted.

They continued to the clearing. Though it was early, several fairies were there already. Laurel recognized Ivy and Primrose. They were polishing the tree stump that held the fairies' beautiful Crystal. Inside that Crystal rested the Chronicles, the book that recorded the fairies' history.

The sight of the other young woodfairies made Laurel recall the last time she'd been in the clearing. She certainly hadn't acted as if she'd be back so soon. She wondered what Primrose would have to say about her return.

That hardly matters, though, thought Laurel. The important thing is to find out how to help the pixies.

As Laurel and her animal friends entered the circle of trees, Ivy and Primrose looked up.

"Laurel!" cried Ivy happily, starting forward. "You're back!" She stopped short when she saw Laurel's worried face. Her eyes took in Laurel's tangled hair and dirty dress.

"What's wrong?" she asked in concern.

"Laurel?" exclaimed Primrose. "Back so soon? You only left two days ago. I thought you were going to be gone for a long time. Forever, even."

Laurel ignored Primrose. To Ivy, she said, "I'm sorry, I don't have time to talk. I must see the Eldest right away."

"I'll come with you," Ivy said.

Leaving Primrose alone in the clearing, they hurried away. Fortunately the Eldest's house was nearby. She'd chosen to build it close to the clearing—and to the Chronicles.

They found the Eldest was also up and about, tending her garden. When she saw Laurel, the old woodfairy almost dropped her watering can.

"Why, Laurel!" she gasped. "Look at you! What on earth has happened?"

"I need your help, Eldest," said Laurel. "Right away, please."

"Of course, of course," said the Eldest. "Do come in. You too, Ivy." She opened her cabin door.

When they were inside, the old fairy said, "Sit down, Laurel. You're completely worn out."

As Laurel sank into a comfortable chair, she realized again how tired she was. But she forced herself to stay awake. Her words tumbled out.

"Oh, Eldest, it's the most awful thing!" she cried. "There's a fire in the forest! It's headed straight for the pixie village!"

Laurel told the whole story. She described the glow in the west and the pixie gathering that she'd left behind.

"Unless something is done quickly, Old Warren will be destroyed," she said. "And we're the only ones who can help."

"How can *we* help?" asked the Eldest in a worried voice.

"I don't expect the woodfairies to go to Old Warren,"

replied Laurel. Apart from herself, no woodfairy ever left the Dappled Woods. They were a shy, gentle people. Even the thought of being away from home frightened them.

Laurel continued. "But maybe we can tell the pixies how to fight a fire. There must be something in the Chronicles about it. After all, we've recorded everything that's happened for as long as anyone can remember."

"I'm very old," said the fairy. "I've seen and heard many things. Still, I know nothing about fighting a fire. Although..."

"Although?" repeated Laurel breathlessly.

"I seem to remember..." The Eldest paused and thought. "Yes, it was when I was around your age, I believe. I remember hearing a passage from the Chronicles about a forest fire. It happened many years ago. Long before I was born."

"Then there is some record!" said Laurel. "Can we check the Chronicles to find out what it says?"

"I'll check, Laurel," said the Eldest. "You need to rest."

"I can't rest!" sighed Laurel. "I've got to get back to Old Warren as soon as possible."

"You won't be of much help to anyone if you're too tired," said the Eldest. She pulled a blanket from the foot of her bed and tucked it around Laurel.

Laurel made one last protest. "Don't forget to wake me the moment you find something. I..."

The rest of the sentence died as sleep overtook her.

～～

When Laurel awoke, warm sunlight was pouring through the window. She sat up, startled. Mistletoe and Chitters, who'd settled beside her, woke too.

The Eldest sat at the table, Ivy leaning over her shoulder. Laurel was surprised to see that Primrose also stood nearby.

"How long have I been asleep?" Laurel asked.

"Not long," said the Eldest. "An hour or two, perhaps. You should try to rest a bit more."

"No, I'm fine," said Laurel, rising to her feet. "Please, tell me what you found. Is there anything about fighting a fire?"

Then Laurel realized that the huge book lay open on the table. The Eldest had brought the Chronicles to her house.

That was most unusual. The woodfairies rarely took the Chronicles out of the clearing.

Perhaps this strange event explained something else Laurel had noticed. Outside the Eldest's cabin, a group of woodfairies had gathered. They were whispering to each other and shyly peeking through the window.

The Eldest saw Laurel's astonished stare. "I asked Ivy and Primrose to help me bring the Chronicles here," she explained. "We've been reading while you slept."

"Did you find out how to fight a fire?" Laurel asked again.

The Eldest stood and looked down at the old, yellowed pages. "Yes," she murmured. "It was as I remembered. There was a terrible forest fire, which the woodfairies managed to put out. Very long ago...Still, it's all here."

"Thank goodness!" Laurel declared. "Tell me what the pixies need to do!"

The Eldest lifted her eyes and shook her head. "You can't do this, Laurel," she announced. "You simply can't. It's much too dangerous."

CHAPTER SEVEN

Advice from the Past

lease, Eldest," Laurel begged. "I have to try. I can't let my friends down. Let me read what it says in the Chronicles."

Laurel hurried to the table to see what the Eldest had discovered. The story was told in neat, careful handwriting. Although the old ink had faded, the words could still be read. In her mind, Laurel pictured the woodfairy who had written this record so long ago. Thank you, she thought. Maybe your words will help my friends.

Quickly Laurel read the story. One dry summer ages and ages past, a fire had torn through the forest. As it burned toward the Dappled Woods, the woodfairies had gathered. After much discussion and advice from other forest dwellers, they came up with a plan. They would build a firebreak—a wide, clear area that flames could not cross.

It was obvious that building the firebreak had been hard, dangerous work. However, the effort paid off in the end. For the fairies finished their firebreak in time. The flames were stopped before they reached the Dappled Woods.

The long-ago woodfairy had been clear in her description of how the firebreak was built. Would it work for the pixies now? Could they save their homes—and themselves?

The Eldest broke into Laurel's thoughts. "Do you see

what I mean?" she asked. "Do you understand why it's so dangerous?"

"Yes, I do," said Laurel. "The pixies don't have much time to build their firebreak. They'll probably still be working on it when the fire reaches Old Warren. If they stay to save their village, they might be putting their lives at risk."

"And so would you, if you're with them," the Eldest reminded her.

"Please, Laurel. You can't go back!" begged Ivy.

"It wouldn't be very smart," added Primrose.

"The pixies may not even be there by now," added Ivy. "After all, they still hadn't decided what to do when you left."

Though Ivy and Primrose continued to talk, Laurel noticed that the Eldest said nothing more. The old fairy just waited for Laurel to make her decision.

Laurel turned to gaze out the window. Her eyes wandered to the beautiful trees, the pure blue sky, and the rainbow of flowers. It was safe and quiet here. The pixies and their problems were miles away.

At last Laurel looked at the Eldest again. "I have to go back. The pixies might have decided to stay and fight. If so, I can't let them down. You do understand, don't you, Eldest?"

For a moment, the others stared at her in concern. Even Primrose looked worried.

Then the Eldest took both Laurel's hands in her own. "It's what I expected. So no more arguments. Do what you must."

Laurel smiled and let out a long, shaky breath. "Now I'd better take some notes about how to build a firebreak."

She reached for her travel bag and took out her journal. For the next several minutes, the only sound to be heard was the scratching of her pencil.

When she finished, Laurel hastily repacked her journal. Ivy stepped forward with a packet of food, which she added to the bag. "Here's something for the journey. I hope you can save Foxglove's village."

"Thank you, Ivy," Laurel said. She shouldered her bag, saying to them all, "I must be getting back."

The Eldest stepped forward. "Promise you'll be careful."

"I promise," Laurel whispered.

As she turned to go, Laurel met Primrose's eyes. A frown wrinkled the other woodfairy's forehead. "Don't do anything foolish," she warned.

Laurel's only response was a tired smile. She walked out of the cabin and past the curious fairies who waited outside.

With Mistletoe and Chitters, Laurel made her way back to the Great Forest. It was full light now, and traveling was much easier. So the three friends made good time.

Along the way, Laurel again saw large flocks of birds. This time she noted other animals passing through the forest as well. All were headed toward Laurel and her friends—and away from the fire.

Several animals called out warnings. An owl, a rare day-time traveler, hooted at them. "Best not go any farther. There's a fire that way."

"How fast is it moving?" Laurel asked.

"Fast enough to frighten me," the owl replied.

A deer, his eyes wild with fear, gave them the same warning.

Laurel asked him, "Have you seen any pixies in the forest?"

"The antler scavengers?" asked the deer. "No. Not today."

As they neared Old Warren, Laurel noticed that the western sky was a sooty black. Below that the earth glowed a bright yellow-orange. It was the fire! The flames had moved close enough to be seen even in daylight.

From that point on, Laurel and her friends didn't stop running until they reached Old Warren. Laurel nearly sobbed with relief. "The pixies are still here!" she cried to Chitters and Mistletoe.

"Still here," agreed Mistletoe. "Though they may not be staying for long."

Laurel saw that the mouse was right. Bags were piled on most of the mounds. Groups of pixies stood here and there, looking at the sky and talking in anxious voices.

There wasn't much time left, Laurel realized. The smell of smoke filled the air, and black clouds nearly blotted out the sun.

"Thank goodness you're back!"

Laurel spun around to find Foxglove and his family rushing toward her.

"We've got to hurry," he went on. "We managed to talk everyone into staying until you returned. Even so, I was beginning to think some were going to change their minds. The fire isn't far off now!"

"Were you able to find anything that might help us?" asked Buttercup.

"Yes. Though it won't be easy," Laurel warned.

"Well, we'd all better hear it," said Bramble.

Laurel nodded and went to the top of the nearest mound. Most pixies had noted her arrival and already drawn nearer. The rest came closer at Foxglove's shout.

"Can we put out this fire?" someone asked.

"I still say it's impossible!" another pixie said. "There's no way to do it."

Laurel swallowed hard. "You're right," she said. "There's no way we can put out the fire."

All the pixies groaned.

"That doesn't mean we have to give up," Laurel added. "We still may be able to save your homes."

"How?" asked a pixie mother.

"We can keep the fire away from Old Warren until it burns out," Laurel replied. "Let me explain."

Laurel took out her journal. In a calm voice, she told about the firebreak the woodfairies had built.

"So that's how you can fight the fire—if you want to stay," Laurel finished. "A firebreak saved the Dappled Woods. One might save your homes too."

"But we all have to pitch in," added Foxglove. "It's going to take every single one of us."

The pixies fell silent, thinking about what Laurel had said.

Finally someone remarked, "It sounds dangerous."

"I agree," called another. "We'd better leave now, while we can." He shivered and pulled his family closer.

More voices joined in the argument. Some thought the pixies should stay and fight. Others disagreed, while still more seemed torn in both directions.

Laurel listened to each speaker. Yet she said nothing. This was a decision the pixies had to make for themselves.

At last the discussion ended and silence fell over the meadow. Those who wanted to leave had convinced the rest. Several families began to walk away, carrying what they could.

Tansy wiggled loose from Foxglove's grasp and darted to her parents. She pulled on her mother's tunic, and Buttercup reached down to pick up her daughter.

Tansy's small voice filled the silence. "Oh, Mama, can't we stay? Even if no one else does?" she asked tearfully.

Everyone looked at the little pixie. As she set her daughter down, Buttercup answered sadly, "No, dear. Either we all stay—or we all go. No one can fight this fire alone."

Tansy stared out at the other pixies, tears rolling down her cheeks. "Please, let's stay," she begged. "This is home!"

Murmurs rose from the crowd. Parents and grandparents glanced at their own children—and their neighbors' children.

A pixie mother cleared her throat. "I'll go get a shovel," she said.

"I'll find some buckets," added another.

"I have an ax and saw," said a third.

As the pixies set into motion, Foxglove moved to Laurel's side. "We're really going to do it, Laurel! For once we're not giving in and moving on." He smiled at her and then sped off to find his own fire-fighting tools.

Laurel shook her head. Her feelings were much more confused than Foxglove's.

"I hope this is the right thing to do," she whispered.

CHAPTER EIGHT

The Battle Begins

hovels, buckets, rakes, axes, ropes, saws, and wheelbarrows. Laurel eyed the pile of tools on the ground. Every pixie family had added something. Even Tansy wanted to help. She'd given her broken belt buckle. "Someone might need it," she explained.

"What next?" Foxglove asked as he dropped a shovel onto the heap.

Laurel took a deep breath. "First we have to clear out all the low bushes and weeds over there." She pointed toward the west. "We need a spot where there's nothing the fire can burn."

"It will have to be long," added Buttercup. "Or the flames will come around it."

"All right. Let's get to work!" cried Bramble.

The pixies collected their tools and moved to the west side of the village. There the grassy meadow gave way to thorny bushes, short trees, and a few giant oaks. Beyond that, the forest grew thick and tall.

"I don't think we can cut those big trees down," Bramble said. "Not before the fire gets here."

"From what I read in the Chronicles, trees that big don't burn easily. Still, we must get rid of everything around them. We need to get right down to the bare ground."

Led by Laurel, the pixies set to work. Some chopped

 down small trees. Others hacked at bushes or raked up dry leaves. Another group carted all the branches and leaves to the far side of the village.

Even Mistletoe and Chitters were hard at work. They ran to and fro, reporting problems to Laurel.

Meanwhile, the air grew hotter and smokier. Yet no one dared rest.

When part of the ground was clear, Laurel called together some of the pixies. "We need to wet down the dirt—quickly!"

Buckets in hand, the group rushed off to the spring. Soon a line of pixies stretched from the pool to the bare patch. Bucket after bucket was passed along the line and poured on the ground.

Laurel nervously paced the entire length of the firebreak. The space that had been cleared wasn't nearly long enough. The fire would easily burn its way around the ends.

"Let me help! I want to help!" came an excited cry.

Laurel turned to see Tansy darting up and down the water-bucket line. She carried her own bucket, which bumped against her legs.

"Please, Tansy," called Buttercup. "You can't help with this, dear. These buckets are heavy, and we have to move quickly."

Laurel saw the look on Tansy's face. She could tell that the small pixie felt useless. Laurel knew how terrible that feeling could be.

"Tansy!" she called. "Come here. I need your help."

Tansy ran to Laurel. Her dandelion wreath had fallen over

one eye, and her tunic was dirty and torn. But she was still full of energy.

"Do you want me to bring you water?" she asked.

"No," said Laurel. "Your mother is right about that. They need to get the water over here as fast as possible. And the buckets are heavy. I'd rather put you in charge of the pile at the other side of the meadow. Make sure everyone brings their leaves and branches to you."

At least this way, Laurel thought, Tansy will be safely away from the fire.

Tansy made a face. "I'd rather pour water on the ground," she said in disappointment. "That's important."

"*Everything* we're doing is important," replied Laurel. "So hurry up now."

With a frown and an angry swing of her bucket, Tansy marched away.

Laurel went back to work. By now she could see flames in the distance, eating away at the underbrush. At least the fire seemed to be staying on the forest floor. The tops of the biggest trees were still green and untouched by flame.

Even so, Laurel grew more and more concerned. They were all working as hard and as fast as possible. Would they finish before the fire reached Old Warren? And if they didn't, could they escape before the flames swept across the village?

She felt as if they'd been chopping, dragging, and digging forever. Yet there was still so much to do.

As Laurel was organizing a second line of water carriers, frightened shouts caught her ear.

"Tansy! Tansy!" the voices screamed over and over.

Laurel spun around in alarm. Posy, Plum, and Petunia were running toward her, tears streaming down their cheeks.

Laurel dropped her shovel and flew to the three pixies. "What's the matter?" she asked.

"Tansy's gone!" cried Posy.

"Don't worry," said Laurel in relief. "I sent her to watch the pile of leaves and branches."

"No! You don't understand," said Plum. "She's not there."

"We saw her when we put some branches on the pile," added Petunia. "By the time we came back again, she was gone."

Now Laurel was worried too. "Did you see where Tansy went?" she asked.

"She was running down the path with her bucket," Posy replied. "When I called to her, she didn't even look around. And...and..." she sobbed.

"And what?" urged Laurel.

"And we were afraid to go after her," finished Posy. She hung her head and started to cry even harder.

"Quick! Which way did she go?" asked Laurel.

Without a word, the three pixies pointed in the same direction—behind Laurel.

Laurel turned, already knowing what she would see. Tansy had taken a path that led toward the burning forest!

A Circle of Flames

hy?" gasped Laurel. "Why would Tansy want to go toward the fire?"

The three girls shook their heads.

"Where does that path lead?" asked Laurel.

"To the stream," said Plum. "It's off in the forest, and she's never gone alone."

"You say she was carrying her bucket?" said Laurel.

As the sisters nodded, Laurel suddenly understood. Tansy had decided to get water. Since no one had allowed her near the spring, she'd decided to get water somewhere else.

But the fire was spreading fast in that part of the woods. And there was no firebreak to stop it!

Laurel dropped her shovel. "Go tell your parents what happened," she ordered.

As the girls ran off, Laurel started toward the path that led into the forest. At a shout from behind, she halted.

"Laurel! Wait!" It was Foxglove, who was charging after her. "Where are you going?" he demanded. "That path leads straight into the fire!"

"Tansy's gone into the forest," Laurel cried. "She wanted to get water. My guess is that she's gone to the stream."

By now Bramble and Buttercup were rushing toward them.

"The girls told us about Tansy," gasped Buttercup. "We

have to find her!"

"You and Foxglove stay and watch over things here," said Bramble.

"No," said Foxglove. "I'm going alone. I know that path, and I can make better time than you. You're both too tired. Besides, the girls are frightened. They need you here."

Bramble and Buttercup looked at one another, their faces worn with worry. "All right," Buttercup gave in. "Hurry," she begged. "Bring her back to us."

"I'm coming with you," said Laurel. "I should have known that Tansy might do something like this."

She could see that Foxglove was about to object. "I won't slow you down," she added. "You know that."

Foxglove nodded. "Let's go," he said. He called to his parents, "Keep everyone working here!"

"We will," promised Bramble. "Be careful!"

Laurel took one last look at the meadow. The fire was getting closer by the minute. That also meant that the danger to Tansy was quickly growing.

Laurel fluttered her wings and flew to catch up with Foxglove. They hurried along side by side, searching for signs of Tansy.

"I've made a terrible mistake," said Laurel.

"What do you mean?" Foxglove asked.

"I should never have suggested fighting the fire. I should have let everybody leave Old Warren. You would have lost your homes. But everyone would have been safe—including Tansy."

"It was our decision to stay," Foxglove said firmly. "Besides, we're going to find Tansy and bring her back." With that, he broke into a run.

Laurel silenced her doubts. She thought only about finding Tansy and returning to help the other pixies.

The two friends slowed as they neared the fire. The roar of flames was louder, while the air was thick with smoke and ashes. Laurel was thankful that Foxglove knew this part of the woods so well.

"How far is it to the stream now?" Laurel yelled, choking back a cough.

"Not much farther," Foxglove shouted back. "Follow me."

Laurel had her eyes half closed to avoid the ash. So she didn't realize that Foxglove had stopped until she ran into him.

"What's the matter? Why—" she started to ask. A blast of heat answered her question. They were facing a towering wall of flames!

"We have to go back!" Laurel shouted. "There must be another way to reach the stream."

"We can't go back!" Foxglove yelled, his eyes wide with fright. "Look!" he cried, pointing the way they'd come.

Laurel whirled around. The fire had spread behind them. They were trapped!

CHAPTER TEN

Lost in the Smoke

aurel and Foxglove spun about, searching for an escape route. There was no way through the flames in front of them. The path behind seemed equally dangerous.

But to the side, there was one area that wasn't in flames.

"Wait here," Laurel said to Foxglove. "I'm going to see if it's safe this way."

Foxglove started to protest. However, Laurel knew there wasn't a minute to spare. She took off, flying above the ground and over the bushes.

The higher Laurel went, the thicker the smoke became. It had been difficult to see to begin with. Now her eyes watered so much from the stinging smoke that she was almost flying blind.

She was nearly ready to turn around when she heard something. It was the sound of rushing water! She'd found the stream! And there was no sign of flames below.

Laurel quickly changed direction and headed back to Foxglove. By the time she reached him, she wondered if she was already too late. Shaken by coughs, her friend had sunk to his knees.

"I found the stream—and there's no fire there!" she cried.

Foxglove eyed the tangled underbrush. He managed to

croak, "I'm not sure I can make it. You go ahead."

"I won't leave you here!" exclaimed Laurel in horror. "Now come on!" She helped her friend to his feet and pulled him toward the bushes.

Together the two struggled through the underbrush. Vines, branches, and thorns caught at their clothes. Because of the smoke, they couldn't see more than a few inches in any direction. So it was a while before Foxglove made a terrible discovery.

"Laurel! I think we're going in circles!" He pointed to some broken branches—and a scrap from his tunic.

Laurel groaned. The nightmare was growing worse by the second.

"I'm going to try to fly above this!" she declared. She untied the sash at her waist. "I'll trail my sash behind me. You hold on to it and keep walking."

Foxglove grabbed the loose end of the sash. Laurel took to the air again, this time gliding just above the bushes. Below her Foxglove held on to the sash with one hand. With the other, he felt his way through the smoke-filled forest.

Laurel worried that they wouldn't reach the stream in time. She began to wonder if they were really going the right way. The roar of the fire had gotten louder. Would she be able to hear the noise of the stream?

Suddenly the sash fell free. Foxglove had dropped his end!

"Foxglove!" cried Laurel. "Where are you?"

"Right here," came the answer. "You did it, Laurel! We've reached the stream!"

With relief Laurel fluttered to the ground. Sure enough, she found herself knee-deep in rushing water.

Foxglove was kneeling on the bank. He scooped up a

handful of water and splashed it over his face.

"Dunk yourself in the water," he said. "That might help if the fire comes closer."

Laurel followed her friend's example at once. The cool water felt wonderful after the heat and smoke of the burning forest.

However, there was no time to relax. "We'd better keep moving," Foxglove urged. "We have to find Tansy and get out of here while there's still a way back."

They started down the stream, both shouting the little pixie's name. They hadn't gone much farther before they got an answer.

"Foxglove! Laurel! Help me!"

Slipping and sliding, they rushed along the muddy bank. Around the next bend, they found Tansy. She was sitting on a rock in the middle of the stream, her arms wrapped tightly around her bucket. Tears tracked down her dirty cheeks, and she was shaking with fright. But she was safe!

With a joyful shout, Foxglove waded to his sister and enclosed her in a tight hug. She hugged him back, holding on as if she'd never let go.

"Oh, Tansy!" cried Laurel. "We were worried about you!"

"You should never have run off like that," Foxglove told her.

"I'm sorry. I wanted to get some water—to help," sobbed Tansy. "Then the fire followed me and I couldn't get back!"

"I know," Laurel said softly. "Still, you outsmarted the fire, didn't you? It was a good idea to get into the water."

That thought made Tansy feel a little better. She gave a noisy sniff and stopped crying.

Laurel dried what was left of the little pixie's tears.

"Everything will be all right now," she said. "We just have to figure out how to get you home."

Foxglove studied the woods behind them. "We can't go back the way we came," he said. "The fire has caught up with us. And there's no point in heading over to the other side of the stream."

He nodded toward the opposite bank, which rose steeply from the water's edge. Water dripped down the rocky cliff, making it dangerous and slippery.

"You're right," said Laurel. "We wouldn't be able to get up there. I guess we'll have to walk along in the streambed."

"Come on," said Foxglove. Still carrying his sister, he began wading through the water. "We'll keep going until we

find a spot where we can climb the bank. From there we can cut through the forest to get back to the village."

So they headed downstream. At first the going wasn't that difficult. However, it wasn't long before the streambed began to narrow. As the banks closed in on them, the water grew deeper—and swifter.

Laurel struggled to keep her balance. Finally, she called to Foxglove, "Do you think we dare try walking along the bank yet?"

Foxglove's gaze went to

one side of the stream, where the bushes still snapped with fire. Then he checked the steep bank on the other side. "We'd better stay in the water a bit longer. The fire seems to be dying out here. It may have completely burned out even farther downstream."

He started forward again. And that's when it happened— he slipped. At once he and Tansy tumbled head over heels into the water.

Laurel cried out and waded after her friends. But before she knew it, she too was knocked off her feet. The current seized her in its powerful grip and spun her away.

CHAPTER ELEVEN

A Wild Ride

aurel kicked wildly, gasping for air. She couldn't seem to make any headway. The stream pulled and pushed at her, batting her around like a bear toying with a fish. One second she bobbed up and was able to snatch a breath. The next she was underwater again.

As the swift water dragged her down, Laurel scrambled to touch the bottom. For a moment, her feet rested on a flat stone. With all her might, she pushed off from the rock and shot upward.

Air! Laurel surfaced, gulping in deep breaths.

Finally, as if it was through playing with her, the current tossed Laurel toward the bank. With heavy arms and legs, she paddled to shore and climbed to safety. Fortunately Foxglove had been right. The fire had barely touched this part of the woods.

Laurel lay on the ground, still panting. But in an instant, she sat up with a start. "Foxglove! Tansy!" she shouted.

There was no reply.

Laurel looked out at the rushing stream. "Foxglove!" she called again. "Where are you?"

A hand weakly rose out of the water just downstream. It was Foxglove! Next a little head bobbed up. "Laurel! Help us!" Tansy yelled.

Both slipped from view as the stream swallowed them again. Laurel caught a glimpse of Foxglove's tunic before the current swept him onward.

She dashed along the bank after the pixies, stopping only to grab a sturdy branch. She'd never have caught up if Foxglove hadn't crashed against a rock in the middle of the stream. With shaking arms, he clung to it. And Tansy, teeth chattering, clung to her brother.

"Don't let go!" shouted Laurel. "I'm coming!"

She pushed the branch into the water toward her friends. "Oh no," she groaned. The branch was too short!

Wildly she looked around for a longer branch. Nothing!

"Just a few more inches," Laurel whispered. Suddenly she had an idea. Her sash had served as a lifeline before. Maybe it would work here too.

She knotted the sash to the branch, then braced herself against a rock. Holding on to the sash, Laurel threw the branch into the water. The current carried it toward Foxglove.

The pixie reached out one arm. "I've got it!" he shouted.

"When I say 'Ready,' push away from the rock and toward the bank," Laurel directed. She dug her heels in. "All right...Ready!"

The branch jerked sharply. Laurel feared she'd lost her friends. But then she realized that what she felt was the current pulling on Foxglove and Tansy.

Hand over hand, she pulled the sash—and the branch—toward her. Her muscles burned with the effort. Yet she didn't loosen her grip until her friends were safe on the bank.

"Are you all right?" she asked.

Foxglove nodded. However, Tansy gulped and burst into tears. "I lost my bucket!" she cried.

Laurel and Foxglove looked at one another and began to laugh. Once they started, they couldn't stop. Tansy was so amazed that she forgot to cry. She just stared at them.

Gradually their laughter died. Then Laurel hiccuped twice, which set Foxglove off again.

"It's not funny," said Tansy in an uncertain voice. "I *did* lose my bucket."

"It's all right, Tansy," said Foxglove. "We're not laughing about that."

"No, Tansy, we're not," Laurel added. "And when everything settles down, we'll find you another bucket."

Laurel rose to her feet and studied the woods. "It looks safe this way."

"We should be far enough south," Foxglove agreed. "I don't think we'll run into the fire. Though it will take a bit longer to reach Old Warren from here."

"We'd better get started."

Foxglove led the way up the bank and through the woods. Now and again, they saw signs of fire in the distance. Flames had blackened trees, twisting and breaking branches. The underbrush was a mass of smoking ashes.

Troubled thoughts filled Laurel's mind. Was this what Old Warren would look like when they arrived?

As they continued, the ground gradually became rocky and bare. With nothing to feed upon, the fire had died out quickly in this part of the forest.

At last they found the path. Tired as they were, they were able to pick up speed on the smooth trail. And before long, they reached the edge of the pixie village.

Across the meadow, they saw the flames creeping nearer the firebreak. The pixies were still hard at work.

Laurel and her friends broke into a run. Even now they might be of help.

Then Laurel gave a gasp of surprise. The firebreak! It was three times as long as when she and Foxglove had left. How had the pixies ever done so much?

On second glance, Laurel noticed the size of the crowd of workers. There were dozens and dozens. Far more than the number who lived in Old Warren.

"Foxglove!" Laurel called. "I don't understand. Where did all these pixies come from?"

CHAPTER TWELVE

In the Nick of Time

oxglove laughed. "Look again!" he said. "They aren't all pixies!"

Laurel studied the lines of fire fighters. "Woodfairies!" she exclaimed. "That can't be! What are they doing here?"

"They seem to be working on a firebreak," said Foxglove. "Which is what we should be doing too." He bent down and picked up his little sister. "Come on, Tansy. Let's get you somewhere safe."

Before he could take another step, a voice called out, "Tansy! Oh, Tansy!"

It was Buttercup. She rushed over and gathered the little pixie in her arms. Tears filled her eyes as she looked at Foxglove and Laurel. "Thank goodness you're safe. All three of you," she whispered.

By now Bramble had come running up as well, with Posy, Plum, and Petunia at his heels.

"We've been so worried," Bramble said. He bent over to plant a gentle kiss on his daughter's cheek.

Tansy's three sisters noisily joined the welcome home. At last Bramble called a halt to the rejoicing. "All right, girls. Please take your little sister over by the brush pile. And keep an eye on her!"

"We will," they cried in one voice. The four trooped off.

Buttercup and Bramble turned back to Laurel and Foxglove. "Thank you for finding her," said Bramble. Buttercup didn't add anything. She simply hugged Foxglove, then Laurel.

"Now we'd all better get to work," suggested Foxglove. "I see you've gotten a lot done."

"Thanks to the woodfairies," said Bramble. "Without them we'd have lost hope."

"I can't believe they came," murmured Laurel. She'd never thought about asking the fairies to help fight the fire. Yet here they were—working as if they'd been battling fires for years.

Laurel's eyes went to the strip of cleared land. It wouldn't be long now before the flames reached it. There was still much to be done.

She hurried to the partly finished firebreak. Woodfairies and pixies alike nodded their greetings, though no one stopped to talk.

So many woodfairies, thought Laurel. Nearly everyone must have come. She could see Ivy digging at the far end of the cleared space. Laurel caught her friend's eye and they traded smiles.

Mistletoe and Chitters were close to Ivy, dragging away leaves just ahead of her shovel. Other fairies—including Laurel's teachers—were working side by side with the pixies. Mistress Marigold had teamed up with Mistress Gooseberry on the water-bucket line. As usual, Mistress Gooseberry was complaining. Yet that didn't stop her from working hard.

But their clothing! It was no wonder that Laurel hadn't immediately recognized the newcomers as woodfairies. Their lovely robes were covered with streaks of dirt. Their hair was tangled and spotted with ash. For once the rest of the wood-fairies were just as messy as Laurel.

Laurel spotted a familiar white-haired figure. It was the Eldest! As old as she was, the woodfairy was pitching in. She was using a thick blanket to beat out sparks that flew from the approaching fire. Laurel recognized the blanket too. That very morning, she'd curled up in its soft folds while napping in the Eldest's cabin.

Laurel hurried to the old fairy's side to help. "Eldest!" she cried.

The woodfairy looked up. "Laurel! You had me worried!" she exclaimed. "Foxglove's parents told me where you'd gone. Did you find the little pixie?"

"Yes—and we brought her back. But what in the world are you doing here, Eldest? You and all the other woodfairies?"

The Eldest smiled. "Just what we should be doing. Helping our neighbors." She smacked the blanket down on more sparks.

"Woodfairies never leave the Dappled Woods," Laurel protested, still finding it difficult to believe. "Except for me."

"Perhaps you weren't the only one who was ready for a change," said the Eldest. She paused to wipe sweat from her face.

Laurel gave the old fairy a grateful smile. "Thank you," she said. "Maybe now there's a chance the pixies will be able to save their homes."

With that, it was back to business. But before long, a familiar voice caught Laurel's attention. She glanced around. It was Primrose, telling everyone what to do—as usual. The woodfairy had organized a large group of pixie children. Now she was shouting out orders: "Let's get those leaves over there!

And that bush! That's right! Keep going!"

The young pixies did exactly as Primrose said. And she worked right along with them. They were clearing the ground faster than anyone else.

Shaking her head in amazement, Laurel went back to her own task.

For what felt like hours, everyone kept at their jobs. They scraped away grass, moved shovel upon shovel of dirt, and dumped buckets of water. Meanwhile, the fire inched steadily closer.

Laurel's back ached, and she could feel blisters forming on her hands. The air was now so hot that it hurt to take a breath. And clouds of smoke were rolling in thick gray waves. Pixies and woodfairies alike coughed and wiped their burning eyes.

In spite of the fact that they were all suffering, hardly a word was spoken. Even Primrose had fallen silent, though she and her team of pixies hadn't let up.

Suddenly someone gave a shout. "Here it comes!"

Everyone stopped to watch the terrible sight. A wall of fire had finally reached the cleared strip of land. Would the fire-break hold the flames back from the village? Or would they all have to run for their lives?

Red-gold sparks shot onto the dirt at the edge of the firebreak. Then fingers of flame clawed at the ground, reaching toward the wait-ing crowd.

But there was noth-ing for the fire to catch hold of. Just a wide strip of bare, wet dirt. The line of flame paused and fell back.

A shout went up: "We did it! We stopped the fire!"

Happy voices echoed the good news. Excited pixies dropped their tools and began to joyfully pound one another on the back. The woodfairies looked a bit stunned by the noisy celebration.

Bramble raised his voice. "Three cheers for the wood-fairies!" he cried.

"Hooray! Hooray! Hooray!" responded the villagers. The woodfairies—even Primrose—smiled shyly in return.

"What do your Chronicles say?" Buttercup asked. "Will the fire burn itself out now?"

"What if it doesn't?" asked someone else.

Laurel stood there helplessly, staring out at the worried faces. She had no idea how to reply. Nothing she'd read in the Chronicles told her the answers to these questions.

"I think we'd better stand guard all night," said Bramble. Foxglove's father was leaning on his shovel. He was plainly about ready to fall over. In fact, everyone looked worn out. Laurel wasn't sure the fire fighters could handle any more. They certainly couldn't stay up all night.

She shot a glance at the Eldest. However, the old fairy merely shook her head. She didn't know what to say either.

Then Ivy—quiet, shy, Ivy—shouted at the top of her voice, "Everybody look at the sky!"

All eyes turned upward. There was a break in the smoke—a break large enough to see that dark clouds had gathered.

The next thing Laurel knew, a huge drop of rain landed on her cheek.

"It's raining!" she cried. She raised her arms and began to

twirl as the drops fell faster and faster.

No one took cover. Woodfairies spread their wings to wash them in the welcome shower. Pixies danced on the wet grass. Children tipped their heads back, catching the fat drops in their open mouths.

And the fire slowly sizzled, sputtered, then died.

CHAPTER THIRTEEN

Welcome Home

y the time the rain ended, everyone—and every-thing—was soaked. But no one seemed to care about being wet. The pixies had gathered in happy groups, hands waving as they relived the day. Children raced about the clearing, with no sign of being tired now.

Under a huge tree, the woodfairies formed a circle of flut-tering wings. They chattered together in high, soft voices. In their own way, they were as excited as the pixies.

"Laurel," Bramble called.

Laurel turned to find Foxglove's entire family hurrying toward her.

"We have an idea," Bramble said.

"We want to celebrate together," explained Buttercup. "Woodfairies and pixies. Nothing fancy," she added. "Do you think the fairies would join us?"

Laurel smiled. "I'm sure they'd love it," she said. "Just invite them."

"Please come with me," Buttercup begged.

With Laurel and Foxglove in tow, Buttercup approached the woodfairies. She stopped in front of the Eldest and cleared her throat nervously. "We pixies would be honored if you'd celebrate with us. After all, if it weren't for you, we probably wouldn't have anything to celebrate."

"We'd be delighted," said the old fairy with a gentle smile.

"Oh, my, um...Why, that's wonderful," said Buttercup. Without another word, she ran off.

Foxglove started to laugh. "You have to understand something," he said. "Pixies don't usually do things together like woodfairies do. So this is a little new to us."

"Just as being out of the Dappled Woods is new to us," said the Eldest. Her eyes twinkled as she added, "It seems that we're all learning something today."

Foxglove and Laurel hurried off to help. Under Buttercup's direction, the pixies carried tables and benches out of their burrows. Next came bowls, plates, and cups. And the villagers raided their cupboards for their tastiest foods.

With the tables set, Buttercup stood back and nodded. Then she swept over to the woodfairies and curtsied. "Won't you please sit down?" she asked.

The woodfairies murmured their thanks and joined the pixies at the tables.

Laurel took a seat next to the Eldest. What would the old fairy think of the noise and confusion of a pixie meal?

But to Laurel's surprise, the Eldest was almost as noisy as any villager. She chatted happily with those around her, laughing at their stories. It didn't even bother her when a small, sticky-fingered pixie climbed onto her lap.

During a quiet moment, the Eldest turned to Laurel. "Your pixie friends care about you a great deal," she said.

"They've been very kind," said Laurel, looking down at her plate.

"So you're happy here?" continued the Eldest.

Laurel raised her head to stare into the warm, dark eyes of the older woodfairy. "Oh, Eldest," said Laurel. "I don't know..."

"What don't you know?"

"I don't know where I fit in," sighed Laurel. "The pixies have been so good to me. But I'm not a pixie. It's just that I can't seem to be the right kind of fairy either."

"There is no 'right' kind of fairy," replied the Eldest. "Every woodfairy is different. And every woodfairy is special."

"Including me?" Laurel questioned.

"Yes, Laurel. Without a doubt. You have a rare gift for understanding others. And a spirit of adventure that we wood-fairies deeply need."

Laurel sat silent for a moment, too stunned to speak. "But...but...you let me leave!" she exclaimed.

"Only because you wanted to," the Eldest reminded her. "Besides, we kept track of you. If you had seemed unhappy, we would have encouraged you to come back."

"You kept track of me? How?" asked Laurel.

The old fairy smiled and nodded toward the far end of the table. Chitters and Mistletoe were sitting there with Foxglove and several pixie children.

Laurel looked from her friends to the Eldest and back again. Suddenly it all made sense. She understood why Foxglove had spent so much time talking to Chitters and Mistletoe. And why the animals had each disappeared for most of a day. They hadn't been exploring the Great Forest after all! They'd been traveling back and forth between Old Warren and the Dappled Woods.

"Foxglove sent word to you, didn't he?" she asked.

"Yes," replied the Eldest. "He gave notes to Chitters and Mistletoe—and they brought them to me. So I knew you were fine."

"You cared that much..." Laurel's voice trailed off.

81

"Of course," said the Eldest. "It's one reason we're here. Yes, we were concerned about the pixies and the forest. But we were also worried about you. We couldn't leave you alone with such a huge problem. We all decided to come and help."

A smile spread across Laurel's face. Even though the sun had set and the rain-washed air was cool, she felt warm. That feeling stayed with her through the rest of the celebration.

The evening drew to a close. The final bite of food had been eaten, the final speech had been given. Several pixies had taken turns thanking the woodfairies. And the Eldest had invited the pixies to visit the Dappled Woods.

Then Foxglove called for everyone's attention. "My wood-fairy friends," he began. "We know you want to return home tonight. So we'd like to guide you safely through the Great Forest." At his signal, several young pixies stepped forward, each carrying a lantern.

Laurel joined the other fairies to say her farewells. Suddenly she felt a familiar tug on her wings. That reminded her that there was one small pixie who needed more than a simple good-bye.

"Where are you going, Laurel?" cried Tansy. "It's almost time for bed!"

Laurel knelt down. "Oh, Tansy, I can't stay here forever."

"Yes, you can," Tansy protested. Tears gleamed in her eyes. "You can stay and be my big sister. Please. Come home with me now."

Laurel hugged the little pixie close. "I can't," she said. "This is your home. Mine is in the Dappled Woods, with the rest of the woodfairies."

She wiped a tear from Tansy's cheek. "Do you remember how you wanted to stay and fight to save your home? How you didn't want to run away?"

Tansy nodded.

"Well," said Laurel. "I just realized something, Tansy. I don't want to run away from my home either."

Laurel knew that the little pixie didn't understand. Laurel barely understood herself. But she did know that she belonged in the Dappled Woods, with the other woodfairies. Even if she didn't fit in as well as she'd like to.

"Will you come back and visit?" Tansy asked, sniffing softly.

"I will," promised Laurel. "And you can come and visit me too." She took Tansy's hand and walked her over to the rest of the family.

"Thank you," Laurel told Buttercup and Bramble.

"We thank you," replied Bramble.

"When you come back," added Buttercup, "put your slippers with the toes pointing in. You're one of the family now."

Laurel smiled. "I'll see you soon," she said.

A gentle voice called to her. "Come on, Laurel." It was Ivy.

"Yes, hurry!" cried Primrose. "It's time to go home!"

Home, thought Laurel. That sounds wonderful to me.

More to Explore

Have fun exploring more about the riches and secrets of the forest. And there are great projects for you to do too!

Floral Headwreath

Create a pretty headwreath like Laurel's out of your favorite flowers.

What you need

- Two stems of artificial flowers, each 12" to 18" inches long. For the prettiest wreath, choose stems that have lots of blossoms.
- Thin wire—floral wire is best, but picture wire will do
- Ruler
- Scissors
- Transparent tape or green floral tape
- Optional: Four one-yard pieces of ⅛"- or ¼"-wide satin ribbon in two colors that go with your flowers

What you do

1. Cut wire in the following sizes: one 15" piece; one 8" piece; four or five 4" pieces. Set the wire off to one side.

2. On a flat surface, lay the flower stems so they overlap. Place the top blossoms of the second stem just below the last blossoms on the first stem. (See the illustration on the next page.)

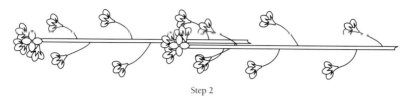

Step 2

3. Using a 15" piece of wire, wrap the two stems together tightly, starting just below the blossoms. Be sure you fold down the end of the wire when you start and then wind around it. When you reach the other end of the wire, tuck it between the stems. If necessary, wrap a little tape around the stems to cover the ends of the wire.

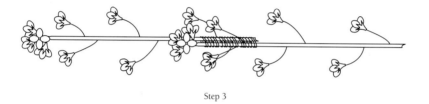

Step 3

4. Bend the joined stems into a circle just big enough to fit on your head, but not big enough to slip down over your face. Holding the stems together tightly where they meet, take the circle off your head.

5. Wind the 8" piece of wire around the stems where they meet. You will need to push the leaves and blossoms aside to do this.

Step 5

6. Use as many 4" pieces of wire as you need to wrap the flowers against the circle. You want the blossoms to stand out a little, so don't wrap them too closely. Be sure to tuck in the ends of the wire so they won't stick you. Use tape if you need to cover the ends.

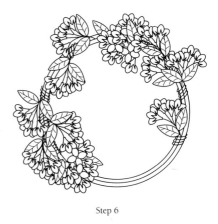

Step 6

7. Tie ribbons at the sides of the wreath if you wish. Use one length of each color on each side. Let the ends hang down.

Other headwreath ideas

- Glue small artificial flowers and leaves to an old head-band. Or use paper flowers that you make yourself.

- Twist pipe cleaners together. Form them into a circle that will fit your head. Then twist to join them at the other end. Use wire to attach small bunches of artificial flowers to the pipe cleaner circle.

Reading the Forest

Laurel knows how to read the messages forest animals leave behind. She can look at a set of tracks and know what kind of animal has been there before her. Sometimes she can even tell if the animal was running, hopping, or just taking a walk.

You can learn to read the forest too. First study the information about different animal tracks. Then head for page 90 to do some tracking of your own.

Rabbit, squirrel, chipmunk, or mouse?

Small rodents (that's their family name) usually leap or jump through the forest. As they do so, they plant their big hind feet in front of their smaller front feet.

A rabbit's tracks look like the ones shown below—only much larger, of course. A squirrel's tracks are similar, but smaller than a rabbit's. A chipmunk's tracks are even smaller. And a mouse's tracks are tiny!

Wolf, coyote, fox, or someone's pet dog?

Members of the dog family leave tracks with four toes and claw marks. The size of the tracks is a clue to what animal made them. A wolf's tracks will be bigger than a coyote's. A coyote's tracks will be bigger than a fox's. And dogs leave tracks of many different sizes. A straight path like the one shown below usually means a wild dog has passed by. Pets tend to wander around more, so their paths aren't as straight.

Mountain lion, lynx, bobcat, or house cat?

A rounded print with four toes like the one below is the mark of a cat. Since cats walk with their claws pulled in, you won't see any claw marks. A mountain lion will leave the biggest tracks and a house cat the smallest.

Birds of all kinds

Birds leave tracks with three long toes in front and one sticking straight out at the back. You can tell the difference between birds that spend most of their time on the ground and those who prefer the trees. Birds like pheasants and turkeys stay mostly on the ground. As they walk, they alternate their left and right feet, like this:

Birds that spend a lot of time in trees, such as robins and chickadees, hop along the ground. So their left and right feet are next to each other, like this:

What about these tracks?

A raccoon's tracks are easy to remember. They look like tiny human feet and hands.

A beaver's front feet look like
hands too. But you can see the
webbing on its back feet.

Deer and other animals with hooves (cows, moose, goats,
and sheep) usually put their hind feet right on top of the
spot where their front feet went. So you won't see two sets
of prints.

More forest-reading tips

The next time you're in the woods or a large park, look for
animal signs. Check the ground for tracks. But there are
other signs you might note as well.

- Do you see a tree with large holes? Perhaps a wood-
  pecker was hungry.

- Can you spot a tree with lots of small holes in the bark?
  A sapsucker has probably been looking for lunch.

- Can you find a hill of seed coatings left over from a
  pinecone? Squirrels like to pile these up neatly as they
  eat.

- Check the bushes. Do some branches look like they've
  been chopped off? If you see an angled cut, a rabbit was
  probably nibbling at a juicy twig. If the end is jagged, it
  was a deer who needed a snack.

- And if you see a tree with its trunk cut all the way
  through, there might be a beaver in the neighborhood.

Test your tracking skills

Now, it's time to go tracking. A lot of animals have walked past this spot: a dog, raccoon, mouse, bird, rabbit, and deer. Can you tell whose tracks are whose?

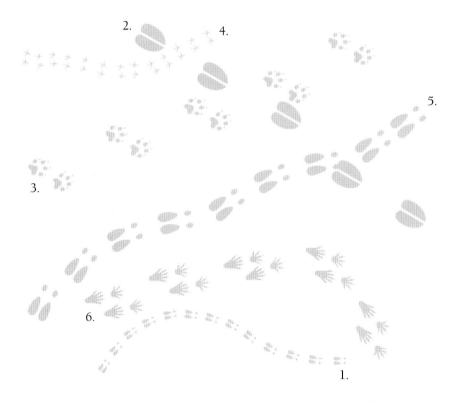

ANSWERS: 1. mouse; 2. deer; 3. dog; 4. bird; 5. rabbit; 6. raccoon

Splatter Painting

Splattering paint can actually be a fun way to make an interesting work of art. Follow the directions below to create a beautiful leaf print. Be sure to do this activity outside or in the basement. It's messy!

What you need

- Large, old shirt or art smock
- Newspaper
- Sheet of white paper
- Piece of corrugated cardboard larger than the sheet of paper
- Large, interesting leaf
- Straight pins
- One to three colors of watercolor or tempera paints
- Disposable pie plates, one for each color of paint
- Old toothbrush

What you do

1. Cover your clothing with an old shirt or art smock.

2. Spread several layers of newspaper over your work area. Cover an area much larger than the paper you will be using. Remember, you're going to be splattering!

3. Place the piece of cardboard in the center of the newspaper.

4. Place the white paper on top of the cardboard.

5. Put the leaf on the white paper. Hold it in place by sticking straight pins through the leaf and paper and into the cardboard below.

6. Pour a little paint into each of the pie tins, one color per tin. If the tempera paint is thick, thin it a little with water. It should be about as thick as spaghetti sauce.

7. Dip the toothbrush in the paint. Shake extra paint off over the pie plate. You don't want too much paint on the brush.

8. With one hand, hold the toothbrush over the white paper. With the other hand, tap sharply on the brush end of the toothbrush. Dots and small blobs of paint will fly off the brush and onto the paper. (You may want to experiment with this technique first, using a scrap piece of paper.)

9. Continue dipping the toothbrush in paint and tapping the paint off. If you want to use more than one color of paint, wait until each color dries before adding the next.

10. Continue until you are satisfied with your splatter art. Be sure you have lots of paint splattered around the edges of the leaf.

11. After all the paint is dry, remove the pins and lift the leaf from the paper. The shape of the leaf will be outlined by splatters of paint.

Stardust Story Sampler

Stardust Classics books feature other heroines to believe in. Come explore with Kat the Time Explorer and Alissa, Princess of Arcadia. Here are short selections from their books.

Selection from

KAT AND THE SECRETS OF THE NILE

Kat and Jessie moved closer to the riverbank. Fine ladies stood on the deck of a tour boat. They wore lovely long gowns and shaded themselves with parasols. On the bank below, barefoot children jumped up and down, begging for coins. Meanwhile, gentlemen in handsome dark suits stood on the dock. Some shouted orders to robed workers.

For a moment, Kat and Jessie watched. Then Kat turned to her aunt. "I know how to find out exactly where we are and what year it is," she said. "See? That man is reading a newspaper. It's bound to have the date on it somewhere."

Kat wandered nearer to the man with the newspaper. As she passed him, she pretended to trip.

"Careful, miss," said the man in English. He reached out an arm to steady Kat.

"Thank you, sir," said Kat. She smiled and curtsied. As she did so, she peeked at the headline. Still smiling, she walked off.

"We're in Egypt!" she whispered when she rejoined Jessie. "And it's 1892! We've gone back more than 100 years!"

Kat couldn't contain herself. She twirled in excitement— and bumped into a worker carrying a barrel.

"Many pardons," the man muttered.

"It was my fault," responded Kat.

As the man went on his way, Kat turned to Jessie. "That certainly wasn't English he spoke—or that I did. Was it...?"

"Arabic?" Jessie finished. "It must be."

"I wish I could figure out how the machine does that," Kat sighed. "I mean how it lets us understand other languages. It's sure a lot easier than studying a foreign language in school!"

"There's only one problem," said Jessie. "You won't remember a bit of Arabic when we get back to our own time."

By now she and Kat had passed the tour boat. Farther down the bank was a long flat-bottomed boat. A few workers were loading more crates and barrels aboard.

"Look at that barge," Jessie pointed out. "It's so full it barely floats!"

"I wonder what all those supplies are for?" said Kat. She and Jessie made their way to one of the workers. Speaking again in Arabic, Kat asked, "Where is this boat going?"

"To the place where we are digging, miss," answered the worker. "To the excavation site at Amarna."

Excavation site! Kat was so excited that she forgot to reply. But Jessie said, "Amarna? Well, thank you for your help."

At that, a tall bearded man who was passing by halted. "You speak Arabic," he said in a strong British accent. "And you are headed for Amarna? Thank goodness, you have arrived at last! And just in time!"

He snatched the traveling bag from Jessie's hand. "Let me carry this for you," the stranger said. Bag in hand, he marched toward the barge. Halfway up the ramp, he called back to them.

"Please hurry!" he ordered. "We are about to leave!"

For a second, Jessie stood frozen, staring after the man. Then she grabbed Kat's elbow and started forward. "Come on! We have to follow him! He's got the time machine!"

Selection from

ALISSA AND THE DUNGEONS OF GRIMROCK

Princess Alissa sighed. "I wish I knew where Balin went and what he's doing now. I miss him. I even miss crabby old Bartok."

Lia laughed. The wizard's parrot had a habit of squawking "Begone!" at visitors—especially Alissa.

"What's really bothering me is that Balin has been gone so long," Alissa said. "I keep checking the tower. Yet there's no sign of him."

"I know," agreed Lia. "And it's strange that he's made two trips in the past month. I thought he almost never left the kingdom."

Alissa's eyes narrowed. "I'm worried," she admitted.

She reached up to touch the locket at her neck. Deep in thought, she ran her fingers over the crescent moon on its surface. More than two weeks ago, Balin had placed the locket around her neck. He'd told her not to take it off until he said so. His face, half-hidden by his flowing white beard, had been wrinkled with concern. She'd begged to know where he was going and why. But Balin had refused to tell her.

"He told me he'd be back in a week," continued Alissa. "Balin never breaks a promise. I know he's in trouble."

"What did he tell you about his first trip?" asked Lia.

"He said an old friend had sent for him," answered the princess. "Someone who needed his help. But when Balin arrived at the meeting place, no one was there. He had no idea who had tricked him. Or why."

"That *is* strange," commented Lia. "Still, don't you think Balin can take care of himself? You've seen how powerful his magic is."

"Remember, he says magic can't do everything," replied Alissa. "Besides, there's something else."

"What?"

"A wooden box is missing from the tower," Alissa revealed. "I noticed right after Balin left for the second time. He kept this strange box on a shelf. There was a dragon carved on its lid."

"Maybe Balin took the box with him," Lia suggested. "Do you know what he keeps in it?"

"No. And I asked him about it more than once. All he'd ever tell me was that the box must never leave Arcadia. So why would he take it with him?"

Lia shrugged. "I don't understand either. Though if he did, I'm sure he had a good reason." With that, she got to her feet. "It's time we got back to the castle."

Alissa rose and began helping Lia pack up their picnic basket.

Just as they finished packing, they heard a loud rustling of leaves overhead. Both girls jumped when something tumbled to their feet, screeching horribly.

Alissa recognized their visitor. "It's Bartok!" she said to

Lia. "Balin must have returned!"

The girls looked around for Balin. There was no sign of the wizard.

Alissa bent closer to check on Bartok. The bird flapped his wings furiously. His feathers were dirty and mussed. And his eyes were wild—even wilder than usual.

She picked up the parrot. "Settle down," she ordered. "Now tell me, where is Balin?"

Bartok glared at her. Loudly he squawked a single word: "Captured!"

"Lia!" cried Alissa in a low voice. "He has to mean Balin! Balin must have been captured!"

STARDUST CLASSICS titles are written under pseudonyms. Authors work closely with Margaret Hall, executive editor of Just Pretend.

Ms. Hall has devoted her professional career to working with and for children. She has a B.S. and an M.S. in education from the State University of New York at Geneseo. For many years, she taught as a classroom and remedial reading teacher for students from preschool through upper elementary. Ms. Hall has also served as an editor with an educational publisher and as a consultant for the Iowa State Department of Education. She has a long history as a freelance writer for the school market, authoring several children's books as well as numerous teacher resources.

JOEL SPECTOR, illustrator of *Laurel Rescues the Pixies*, was born in Cuba and moved to Queens, New York, when he was 12 years old. He graduated from the Fashion Institute of Technology in New York City and began his art career as a fashion illustrator.

Mr. Spector has illustrated many books and other materials. He provided illustrations for a Japanese series based on the Anne of Green Gables books. The series was intended for use in teaching English in Japan—where Anne is an extremely popular character.

Joel Spector lives in Connecticut with his wife and their four children. His oldest son, Max, was the model for Laurel's friend Foxglove.

PATRICK FARICY, the cover illustrator, was born and raised in Minnesota. He began his art education there, studying communication design, illustration, and fine art at the School of Associated Arts in St. Paul. He completed his studies at the Art Center College of Design in Pasadena, California.

Since graduating in 1991, Mr. Faricy has been living in California and working as a freelance illustrator. His clients include Coca-Cola, Kellogg's, Busch Gardens, and Warner Brothers.

When he's not painting, Patrick Faricy spends his time writing and playing music, going to the movies, and talking with friends. And he is always on the lookout for something new and different to add to his frog collection!